TRUE CONFESSIONS

RICHMOND B. ENGELKE

SUM OF ALL REASONS

The face of one's faith is a fantasy into the reality of life. Chosen words of biblical thoughts are the weakness within the human's race. Yet the power of being a chosen leader is also a powerful soul. Willing to control the thoughts and minds of innocent souls. Who are victims of their fantasies?

Strange days carry the unknown factors. Living the life of a police officer. The early morning hours after the sun rose. Rain began pouring and rolling down the windshield. would also change an unknown portion of his life. Buried in a cemetery surrounded by a church. Also, housing a peaceful complex church and a home for the priests living inside of a sanctuary. Outside was a compelling a story i with unknown facts and lies. Unexplained reasons to cover up the past.

John Holmes stood beside his self. Studying the tombstones. Staring back at him. Dripping cold wet rain rolled over his eyes. A lifeless young child lay there alone in the rain. Unnerving fear came over his emotions. The child was lifeless and alone. One by one tear drops rolled out of a man's broken soul. John Holmes could not swallow the spit inside of his mouth. His tears caused him to gag and choke of the sight of a lifeless child covered with rain. Stepping back from the horror of a lifeless child. Who could not ask for any type of hope or forgiveness? Rain splattered off the plastic raincoat to the sound of thunder. Slipped it off. Placed over the body of a lifeless child. Stood still praying for forgiveness. John Kneeled down placed his hands in the mud. Lifted his head as tears of sorrow and pain drifted over his cheeks. Screamed out loud. "Where the hell are you God? Why did you take this child from me?"

Everyone stopped. Before anyone noticed a group of police officers had kneeled in the mud. Recited the lord's prayer. No one moved until John Holmes stood up.

The echo of silence was a sharped edge knife cutting the surface of hell.

Emily witness the heart and souls of full-grown men. Sharing their dignity and honor for one lone child. Who died without the compassion of love and hope? She held the tears drops within her heart and soul in that one moment. Emily walked in the rain. Kneeled on one knee with a body bag. Buzz laid his paw on the lifeless child and howled.

In one short moment of life. The compassion of honor and love gave honor to a child.

Emily placed a raincoat over John Holmes's shoulders. "Go home John. You suffered long enough today."

John Holmes never spoke a word. Soaking wet man marched away. Every police officer stood erect to honor his compassion and sorrow.

Emily remembered the strong will police officer. Who shared his compassion with her on the doorstep again? Today she witnesses a broken man in the need of hope. Emily whispered. "Never have I seen. So much heartache and pain in one person's life. You saved my life. I am going to save your life and dreams too."

In the dark shadows of broken souls. Life held no one accountable. Time was an empty vacuum. Shades of sunlight created a reflection of lost souls. It was the only reflection from the sun light high above the cemetery. The spirit of angels was sentenced to face the empty souls lying beneath the sole of shoes walking over them. Voices of the victims came to whisper from the depths of time. Hoping for the darkness of sin to disappear. Allow the light to shine down on their lost souls. Yet to be found under the ground in shallow graves without hope.

John Holmes turned back around to search the emptiness. He felt inside of his thoughts. Tears rolled one by one. Out of the corners of his eyes. Hands trembled as he searched for a reason why? For once in his life. Realize he was alone to face the conflict in his life. Nowhere in the depths of his heart. Could he find the words of compassion and hope? The one true love of his soul was gone forever. Walked down a slippery wet slope toward his car. Drove away to face the lost moments in life alone.

Emily stared down at Buzz. Crying out loud. Hoping John Holmes would come back too. It was the first time Emily ever saw Buzz suffer and cry. For one time in life she saw two broken hearts crying out for each other. She turned back to tell everyone to continue the search for evidence concerning the child. "Listen everyone. Please search for any evidence. Concerning this child. I am going to check on John Holmes. Please forgive me. Do not linger long in the rain. Go home as soon as possible please." Without another word. Emily walked away. Buzz walked with her. Opening the back door. Buzz jumped up and laid down. Driving away to search out the emptiness inside of John Holmes heart. Passing Campbell on the way out.

Campbell realized that John Holmes was gone. Something must have happened at the cemetery. No one was around to inform him. Decided to turn and around. Hoping to find John and Emily back at the office.

Emily felt an uneasy emotion ticking out loud in her thoughts. Every second of her life ticking away in fear. Thinking John Holmes may have decided to end his life. The weight upon her thoughts and soul. Pushed the accelerator pedal downward. Fear engulfed her imagination. Thinking about the toughest hard nose police officer in her life. Was distraught enough to take his own life? Sudden stop. Without any hesitation Buzz jumped over her lap. Golden haired dog ran pawing at the door and howling.

John Holmes had been staring at the 9milmeter on the table. Sudden shock and sound of Buzz howling. Forced him to get up and open the door. Emily was jumping into his arms and Buzz jumping all over him. A voice of hope whispered to his heart and soul. It was a thirteen-year old girl. Sitting on a door. A calm soft voice of love captured his thoughts. In one instant John heard a sound of compassion. A voice whispered. "You saved my life. I felt like I could not let you waste your life. I was so scared of losing you." Tears rolled her cheeks.

"For the first time in a long time. I heard an angel talking to me. I never expected the angel to be you. I wanted to die. After seeing that young child. Staring back at me. It was not about Mick. It was about me. I finally ran into a wall. It hurt so bad."

A tiny finger touched his lip. "You were never alone. Buzz cried out for you. The pain in his heart and soul called after you. I found myself alone for a second time. I was not going to lose you. You are the only person. I ever think about. I want you in my life." Emily held onto him. She finally found the reason to live too.

John Holmes finally realized. Life was not about pain and sorrow. It was the passion of life itself. The life he once loved was gone. But an angel found a way to guide him to another one. Into his miserable life of being alone and helpless. Mick had jolted him the same way. Now the compassion of a child. Who grew up to be a woman? Did the same thing to him. It seemed as if Mick knew all along. She had found the perfect woman for him. "Can you stomach a hard nose old fool lady?"

"Can you share that old hard-nose love too?"

John Holmes stared down at Buzz. "How about you Buzz? Do you think? We could be partners too."

Buzz sat there staring at John Holmes. John Holmes spoke. "Emily give him a treat. I smell. The mud is not helping my appearance." John Holmes walked away to take a shower.

Emily flipped Buzz a treat. "Well Buzz, what do you think? Should we keep him?" Buzz barked at her. "I assume that is a yes."

Buzz walked over and crawled up into a chair.

"It seems. Someone has found a home. How about you?"

"I think. I could get used to having you around. What about me?" Placed her arms around his neck. "Well?"

"I don't think. I have a choice. I lost my chair, found a beautiful woman to protect me. Emily, you and Buzz saved my life. I made up my mind to end it. Somehow fate intervene. When you touched me and spoke? I found a reason to care and live. I am sorry. I never wanted you see and find me like this. I lost everything today. That little child broke my heart. I was suddenly alone. Everything overtook me. I had to run. I lost everything in that one moment. My life was worthless. I fell to the ground. No one or anything ever mattered to me at that moment. I was ready to die. I am sorry. You had to see me like this." Tears rolled the cheeks of a broken-hearted man.

"You were never alone. Every officer out there felt just like you. They all kneeled and recited the lord's prayer and stood up. Silently stood still to honor you. I cried. Everyone cried for your loss. Your compassion. You gave all of them the desire to solve this murder. I am so proud of you. You found the compassion and love to share this with everyone. They honored you." Emily wiped away the tears. Rubbed them in her palms. To remind herself to cherish life.

Perhaps the darkest moment in life. Is the prophesy of life. No one can explain the unknown will of the unseen miracle of life. Two people bound by the words of a dying man. Found and shared the prophesy of life. Sun rose from a fiery red sky. John Holmes reached over and found a big bundle of fur. Snoring out loud. Surely it was not a nightmare. A soft voice whispered. "Get out of bed. Time to get ready for work. Breakfast is almost ready." Emily slammed the door to wakeup Buzz. Opened it. Buzz leaped to the floor and ran past her for breakfast. "Get up John. Buzz will leave nothing."

The early morning breakfast stirred the thoughts of John Holmes. After his mental break down yesterday. A different man approached life with a kin sense of life. The emptiness of life no longer claimed his lost soul. Instead a man, who claimed he could ride to and from hell. Found the temptation of life to be more difficult than dying. A woman and a dog saved a lost soul.

Emily rolled down the back window so Buzz could feel the wind in his face. She admired the confidence of a broken man had returned. She stood beside John Holmes in front of the police station. Admiring the collection of people walking by. For some reason, the faces of guilt outnumbered the innocent victims. Prying into the minds of people passing by the station. A sigh of relief came with the sound of a missing soul in the investigation of one child.

A third car pulled up and parked. Emily glancing over at the windshield. John Holmes stood still and found the missing link, the person inside of it. Was one Officer Campbell. Who survived the past life of his father's failure? Hoping to find hope in being reassigned to John Holmes. Stepped outside. Stood still long enough to admire John Holmes. Also felt the same sorrow about him standing in the rain. Protecting a dead child from the rain. Stood silent in the pouring rain. "Good morning John and Emily." Offered Buzz a treat.

"Campbell, did you go to the cemetery yesterday?"

"Yes sir."

"Well we are going back this morning. You are driving." John Holmes smiled. Buzz paid little attention and ignored all of them. Emily open the door and Buzz jumped in. Not much of a conversation was spoken.

John Holmes stepped out. Walked straight up the hill. Stood silent reflecting on his failure from the day before.

Emily stopped Campbell. "Let him alone. He is searching his thoughts and soul right now."

Buzz ignored everyone. The keen sense of smell decided to walk around the crosses and tombstones. Emily quietly observed Buzz at work. "Stand still Campbell. Let Buzz wander around. He is searching for something."

John Holmes turned his attention to a window above him. Remembered seeing a man. Standing at it. The same figure stood in the window once again. Whatever the reason was? John Holmes understood the vision of one man. Could it hold a key to the hold mystery of life and death. Why there were so many unknowns? On the other hand, John Holmes observed the dark black nose at work. Emily observed Buzz's movements for telltale signs of death. Sniffing around graves for something. Buzz found a scent of death was tracking it down. Patiently tracked the scent. Buzz slowed down his movement. Something was amidst. Emily waited patiently for the one final movement to happen. Tracking back to the first body. Where it was discovered. Finally Buzz stopped. Three graves back from the body of the day before. Sat down on top of a grave. The ominous sign of death appeared.

Emily walked closer and stopped by John Holmes. "John, turn around. Buzz has found a sign of death."

John Holmes turned around. The symbol of death appeared. The scent of death reared up the fatal attraction. No one wanted to appear. Silence filled the air. No one spoke a word. Death created a morgue of another lifeless soul. It was an unwanted attraction between the boundaries of heaven and earth. The unholy reflection stood between the searchers and the demons of hell. Yet an angel's presence belonged to the scent of a loyal dog. "Buzz, your sniffer is bad luck and god sent you my friend."

Emily teased John to lighten the moment. "I have never seen two cops created from the same mold. You two can sniff out the worse situations. I bet you two came from the litter."

John Holmes smiled. "I guess the job of the trainer requires a bit of insanity. But the reality. It is as close to hell as I want to be. Wonder why anyone would want to do this to a child. Somehow, my instinct is doubting the reason and outcome. Look at the window above. Those are the eyes of one of god's servants. Even in his thoughts and prayers. He has begun to question our existence down here."

Emily and Campbell stared directly up into the window. Within a few minutes the presence of God's attendant disappeared.

"One thing is for certain. His eyes are beholding to one master. The prayers for a dead child are covered by the shadows of his on sins. Makes me wonder about one of god's trustful servants."

Campbell spoke a few solemn words. "Lord forgive our thoughts and sins. The child before us deserved a better life. May you take his soul to a better place."

"Campbell, this is a better place. Except for the death of the young boy. It will ring hollow long before justice is served." John Holmes cast doubt on Campbells thoughts and prayer. The reason for seeing it. Was a way of peace for the unwarranted death of a child. "Let's go see, what is Buzz is alarmed about."

None of them took notice of the lone figure up above. Who reappeared in the window?

The search for death's next companion was washed away from the rain and tear drops too. One silent lone figure observed the devil's work. Admiring the culture of arch angels disguised as the police. All of them working to discover the cause of death buried beneath the ground of shallow graves. Nothing seemed to matter to the dark shadow of soul witnessing it all unfold. The listless body buried beneath the guardian of his soul.

Emily called Buzz off.

Yet he would use the words of God and ask forgiveness for their child like sins. "Bless the victims within our garden of stones. Forgive the ones, who trespass on the dead. They know not or why? The lord exposed the search. Only to seek the darkness of the devil himself. May God forgive their sins. For they not what evil is before them."

John Holmes took a moment to see if the man in the high tower above him had returned. Truth between death and life stood over his thoughts. Up inside of the tower a lone figure anguish over the thought of one single man stood between heaven and hell. The black suit cloaked the darkness between his prayers as a servant of god. The moral soul of a priest was being choked by a white collar. Admiration found a mortal man. Who chose to stare up at him without any hope and suddenly signed the cross?

Emily witnessed the courage of one single man. Who did not hide his fear of the power of god? "John, you tempt the arc angel of life and death, why?"

"For one simple reason. Who is standing above us? The arch angel of god is also tempting us to challenge his authority. I refuse to be humbled by his manners or his black cloth suit."

Campbell tried to shake off the insults. "John, why are you tempting the priest?"

"For the same reason you feel like. You must be humble to respect him. I treat him as my equal." John spit at Campbell's shoes. "Ever wonder about the confessions of killers? I have done it several times. But for some reason the voice cracks. Every time I hear. I am innocent. That same curse is written in the sins of the church too."

"Campbell, reality is the only true value of a sin. It is not covered by the bible. It covered by the law and justice. Next time a criminal begs for god's forgiveness. Ask the victim. Who did not survive, why?" Emily chose to defend her boss.

"I was taught to respect the church. But by your conclusions and past views. I am being forced to perform an act of a sin. I would not judge the dignity one's religion as a pass to commit murder or rape of a child. Not even in front of you right now." Emily understood the value of being forced to do unwarranted acts. She protected and hid from her past.

John Holmes stepped in between the two of them. "Campbell leave your faith at home. The case before you is the reason. You are here. I gave you a second chance. Do not let me down."

Campbell stepped back and let his personal demeanor go away. Tried to regain his self-confidence. The one and only reason he was here in the first place. Realized his youthful past would always haunt him one way or another. "I am sorry. I seem to have forgot why? We are here. It is the death of a child. Not my judgment of right or wrong concerning someone's faith."

Emily laughed at the choir boy confession. "Oh Campbell. No one passed judgment on you. It was your boss telling you to chill out. This is a crime scene." Buzz passed judgment on all of them and barked. "Looks like the warden wants some respect."

"Time to move on up toward the hill. Mister Buzz has rattled our cages once again. That dog is smarter than we are. He takes care of business." John Holmes enjoyed the compassion of Buzz's nose and his cry for help.

Emily rushed up the hill. Gave him a treat. To calm down her emotional detective. "Good boy. I am sorry. Please forgive me."

Both men laughed. Buzz took complete control of all their emotions. John Holmes wanted to turn around. Even as he wondered about the new find. Even if there was no body. But Buzz had dug at the soul of a man by a grave. "Campbell go get the shovels and rakes. I think we have a serious new problem."

"On my way." Campbell did an about face.

"John, what do you think?" Emily knew, what to expect. Buzz did his job.

"I am afraid of what we will find. This may be the beginning of something larger. I hope. It is not a child's body." John Holmes felt remorseful. Being a detective never stopped him from doing his job. Sentimental hope for life was also a reason to fear it. Usually the answers would come back with nothing but bad news? The pouring rain had already delivered a body. John Holmes turned away to avoid a conclusion. Pacing back and forth. Trying to find a calm moment of hope. His nerves shook the very soul of hope inside of him. Sentimental emotions came with the same determination as hope did. The gut feeling was also another reminder. That the death of his wife was something that needed to be put to rest. For so many years, the haunting death and mourning served only as a reminder. Wiped away one last tear. Time to cover the memories of his past. Faced Emily. "I needed to make a decision. Sorry but it required me to move forward. Forgive my distraction."

Emily realized. John Holmes decided to bury the past images and thoughts of his wife. The actual memories of his wife's death needed to be put to rest. The tears also were a painful choice to handle. Emily took his hand. Held it close to her heart. Whispered to him. "Her love will remain in your heart. Always think of her life. She will always be with you." John Holmes smiled. Held her hand to comfort her thoughts and compassion. An odd emotional moment caught him off guard.

John Holmes quietly smiled. Turned to face Campbell carrying a hand full of tools. "Okay bring them over here. Buzz please sniff at it one more time."

Emily lead Buzz over to the grave site. Buzz laid down on top of it.

John Holmes sighed. Taking a long hard deep breath and sighed. "Campbell bring me a shovel and a rake. I will start the dig process." John Holmes slowly move the particles of the dirt. Pushed the topsoil and rake it back and forth. Moving it side to side. Brushing it off to the surface of the grave. Wet sloppy mud refused move or co-operate without some sort of help from the rake. Slowly it began to move and allow the dig to continue. Kneeled on his knees. Began to brush it side by side. Moving it inch by inch. No one spoke to John Holmes. Buzz sat down beside him. Patiently waiting for a body to be found. John Holmes hit pieces of wood. Expecting to find a shallow grave with a body inside of it. The planks of wood exposed his desire and weakness to continue. Emily relieved him. To discourage the painful memory of his wife. John Holmes kneeled beside of her on his hands and knees. Pushing the mud away, pulled one of the planks loose. Exposing a body of a small child. School uniform tattered and rotten from the pages of time. Unfortunately, the angelical child's skull had been bashed. Tears of sorrow and hate created an unforgiving enraged mad man. John Holmes threw the rake across the rolls of crosses. "I will find this son-of-a-bitch." John Holmes looked straight up the window. It was dark. No one stood peering down into his soul.

The evening set in and tortured one single man with a dark soul. Flood lights spread across the sinister landscape surrounded by crosses. Except there was no shining light from heaven above. The investigation of one child lead to another long-forgotten child. John Holmes would have no excuses for leaving. The forbidden crimes from the past and present crossed an abyss of time. Represented a fraction of someone's desire to molest and murder little boys. The ordain order of practicing and preaching God's word. Would be the first ones to be investigated. John Holmes stood in the middle of mud puddle observing Emily and Buzz. Deep down in his heart. Realizing the anger took away his judgment. "Emily bring Buzz in. Listen everyone here. Go home and sleep. I expect you here tomorrow after you have had a good night's sleep. Campbell, you over see the night watch. Select five officers to protect the sight. By seven in the morning I will relieve you. Spend the rest of the day off. Come on Buzz and Emily. I will drive you home."

John Holmes wondered about the past few days. How long would someone do this crime? Why were the victim's children?

Searching the complex riddles of the past. When and where did death begin to intersect with the past and the present day? Unable to separate his thoughts. The past created more confusion. The answers he wanted to hear were not there. The car door opened. Buzz slide in onto the back seat. Laid down and slept.

Emily yawned. "Please take me home to get clothes. I prefer to stay at your apartment. I don't want to be alone tonight."

John Holmes smiled. "I could see it in your eyes. This is my fault. I let my anger take control and get the best of me. I am sorry for it." John handed her a dry blanket. "I will wake you. When I get you home? To get the things you need. Now go to sleep."

Emily closed her eyes. Before she fell asleep. She peeped out from under the blanket to admire his love and kindness. It was a wonderful emotion of concern. He shared with her.

The early morning hours hovered over the dawn of time covering a new day. The scent of breakfast circled the morning air and woke up a man. Who had long forgotten about the scent of food? That once covered his own kitchen. When was the last time he smelled fresh coffee? The impulse and gut reaction told him. He had overslept. At least he thought about it. But a humming sound coming from a musical chef changed his mind. "Good morning, did I oversleep?"

"No. I called Campbell. Told him to explain to the morning crew. That you would be late. For them to resume my work. I thought you needed to rest. The stress and anger overtook your emotions last night. Now go get a shower. Look respectful Officer Holmes. By the way you do not look like you felt last night."

John Holmes smiled. "Been a long time sense a woman. Told me to clean up my act."

"Hurry up before Buzz decides on seconds. Right now. He is outside." Emily pushed him toward the shower. John Holmes enjoyed the strong-willed woman in his kitchen. Just maybe it was the emptiness inside of his life. Telling him to move on from the past. The same emotional thought of being alive changed a part of life long forgotten. Enjoyed having Emily around. Could have sworn. He saw a slight twinkle in her eyes too. Emily heard a sound in the shower. He was humming a song. She laughed. Realized he had feelings. She enjoyed the thought of making him feel like a new man. At last she finally found his lost emotions.

Sound of water and humming stopped. A well-dressed man came out in jeans and sweatshirt. "Well, I thought I should be prepared for work today."

Emily smiled. Escorted him to the table. Placed a plate on the table with hot coffee. Placed a second plate on the floor. Buzz wasted little time. Began eating breakfast alone. "Please excuse me. I need to go shower. Prepare myself for work. I enjoyed your compassion last night. You have a wonderful heart and soul, John." Smiling as she danced away to the shower. The connection between the two had made a connection. Emily reappeared. She wore a pair of jeans and a blouse. A bit tight which allowed her curves and beauty to show. "Alright boss. I am ready for work. How about you Buzz?"

Buzz sat staring at a perky woman with a smile. Yet it never distracted from his norm. John spoke. "I am glad my forensics expert is so attractive. I sure forgot. How wonderful it is to have a woman around. Shall we attack the world once more my lady?"

Emily took his arm. "You are the boss. I am happy to appease my boss. Shall we?"

Emily and John Holmes arrived at the cemetery. John Holmes stood silent for a long period of time. Staring up at the lone figure. Whom seemed fascinated with the police officer below. Yet John was also fixated on the work below? John Holmes stared back up to acknowledge the man in the tower. Emily walked away with Buzz. She understood the power play between the two adversaries in the game of death. Being played before her eyes. The priest seemed to lack empathy. Yet the creation of god's subject was subject to being reviewed by the police officer in charge. Challenging his authority and power. The strange darkness of death created a cloud of distrust between the two men. Emily considered the unknown factor between the two of them. One was a police officer and the other was a priest. It seemed that power was an issue. "Come on Buzz. We have a long day in front of us." Buzz slipped away. Began searching for a cadaver. Unfortunately, the keen sense of his abilities. Produced the unwanted thoughts of Emily's profession.

John Holmes realized. The priest had walked away. A sign of power for him temporally. Stood erect and silent. Admiring Buzz and his master. Decided to wait until Emily required his assistance. Walked toward the discovery graves from last night. The two bodies long removed. The conscience of death also played a part in his emotional break down the night before. A new day relieved the break down. Determined to overcome the night before. John walked up to the graves. Cast his eyes upon a long roll of graves. Why would so many children? Why would they become victims? Memory of Alan Poe seem to infect his thoughts. A professional serial killer without a conscience. He wondered about the strange encounter between the two of them. How could a man be a serial killer? Have been an endearing compassionate man toward a child? The lingering thought proved one thing for certain about Allan Poe. Changed the life of a child and turned her into a compassionate lady. Emily was willing to retrace the past and fine closure for a lot of parents. Only one thing remained. It was beginning to ignite a fire inside of the church. Strangest part of it was controlled by the church itself. No one inside would dare to come forward and answer a few questions. John Holmes considered the daily environment and the depressing life of being a witness for god's salvation. Why would a priest or church worker even offer any assistance to the police? It would require a miracle in god's presence to over-turn his judgment. Where would the proof come from? To file charges against the church.

Emily casually strolled by Buzz. Seemed to have lost interest is the saga of death. Figured it would easier for Buzz to be still and silent. Wagging his tail. Staring down at John Holmes. Emily admired the odd kinship between a four-legged dog and the other one standing casually on two legs. Stopped to admire John Holmes. Saw the anguish his stare. Wondered about his thoughts. Admiration turned to the well-being and conscience of the hunter. Desire to find answers from the one person. Hiding behind the cloak of god and the church. Buzz sat down beside of her. This time he began to sniff the grave. It was unusual. Buzz dug at the soil. Emily pulled him back from the grave. A sudden shock struck her eyes. Buzz brushed enough soil to expose a fresh grave. She screamed. John Holmes was startled by her scream. Ran directly up to the hill to the of the side grave. Kneeling to push away the soil. Emily cried. The pure innocence of a child in a fresh grave. John Holmes stood still. Lifting him up from the grave. Held him close to his chest. "Emily stop now. Please go back down the hill. Take Buzz and wait inside the car."

"Detective Holmes. Please let me finish." Emily picked him up. Wiped away the tears. "Just stand by me please. This is difficult right now. I need your support and love too. I am afraid."

John Holmes realized. The two of them loved each other. "Don't worry. I will be right here. You have my word. If you get shaky. I will finish it until you regain your emotions. I promise."

Emily's hands trembled. But the compassion of her soul controlled the weakest moment in her life. Proved her courage and will were both there. The tedious passion of love moved her forward inch by inch. Slowly brushing the dirt from around a blue-eyed boy. Admired his sandy blonde hair in a motherly sort of way. Casually rushed away the dirt from around his body. The tips of her fingers closed his eyes. Silently prayed and cuddled the silent child's soul. Protected an angel from the prying eyes of the world. She gingerly cleaned up his face and hands. Wiping away every ounce of the particles of dirt on his tiny body. Slowly unzipped a body bag. John Holmes kneeled. Helped Emily to pure innocence of a young boy into a dark body bag. Emily spent-stroking and brushing particles of dirt out of his hair. The grace of tears drops dripped onto his face. A slight bright light from the sun created a tiny rainbow of love. In a strange sort of way. The tear drops rolled over the edges of his cheeks. John Holmes folded the cover over his body. Slowly zipped it up. Emily sat down by Buzz and cried. Police officers removed their hats. Six officers walked up the hill. Gently lifted him up. Marched the tiny soul down the hill. Placed the body inside of an ambulance. Close the door and stepped back saluting the child.

John Holmes witness the loving passion of grace unfold. Sworn vengeance upon this dark moment in his life. Turned his attention back to Emily. "Come with me. I think you need to leave. I will drop you off at my apartment. Take Buzz home too. When I have finished here today. We will sit down and talk about it."

Emily took his hand. John Lifted Emily from her knees. Walked side by side with her down the hill. John Holmes opened the door. Explained to an officer on duty. He would return. Thought it was best to take Emily home for the day.

Compassion holds the truth. Words are spoken to ease the pain inside of the heart. Emily felt her pain and heart break.

About an hour later. John Holmes stepped back into the cold world. Where no child was safe from death. Walked up the hill. Stared down at the empty grave of a one child. Who took away his heart and soul? Whispered. "I will seek the truth. No one will be forgiven for this crime."

Campbell walked up behind him. "I could not sleep. Thinking about all the bodies were children. Inside of this graveyard. Protected by the church."

John Holmes turned around and spoke. "Emily is at home. She was overcome by the body of a young boy. Thanks for coming back. Come on with me. Time to enter the halls of worship. Seek the voices of god's testimony." Without any hesitation walked down the hill. Pushed the wooden door open. Inside the halls of Jesus's Kingdom. Purity and innocence covered up by the sins of the past. Somewhere in the darkest moments of life. A sin was covered up by God. A priest stepped forward to greet them. "How may I help you?"

John Holmes flashed his identity. "Please advise the head priest to come down and speak with us."

The young priest stepped back. "As you wish. Please wait here."

Turned his attention back to Campbell.

"Well, I guess. We understand each other for now. Oh, one more thing. Walk around the inside of the chapel. Check the exit doors. I would not want to miss him. Should he decide to vacant the church?" John felt no remorse for the man. Who stood admiring the deadly scene from a window? Never once did he come or say a prayer or ask to help in the investigation. John almost fainted.

The curtain behind the door opened. A tall dark hair haired lanky man appeared. "I heard your conversation from behind the curtain. Why would I not convey a message to you. It is your investigation. Not mine. I suggest. You respect the wishes of the church. Whatever is happening within the walls is my business. The hollow ground outside is for the public. We tend only to god's temple. Not the wicked souls walking about here in the night or the past. If a crime was committed. You should do your job not mine." The priest turned around to leave.

"Quite a display of power. Have you ever considered the truth? Your saintly posture above the cemetery. Is like a vulgar condemnation of the devil laughing at us. Are you the devil or a saint?" John Holmes never allowed anyone to insult or deny a crime. "My convictions of religion are determined by faith alone. So, judge me for who I am. Not for your mere mortal wellbeing as a priest."

"Quite a sermon for a mortal man. Whose convictions of criminal intent is on display. Have ever considered confessing the sins. You speak of before questioning my morals for Christ's work?"

"So. A simple sermon from a mortal man. Threatens your power over me. I am just one man. I have no desire to tell you about my morals or character. I asked you questions. You spoke and judge me. Tell me about the morals of murder. As I stand there day after day. Watching the innocent souls of children. Who were raped and murder? Tell me where is? Jesus right now!"

"I have never pasted Judgment on you. I am a mere mortal soul. Doing God's work. So, forgive my presence. I have work to do." The priest walked away in silence.

John Holmes held his thoughts in silence. Yet the moral argument of one priest and man representing the law, was a standoff of power. No one gave an inch in the war of compassion.

"You see Campbell. The difference between religion and crime is the convictions of two different men."

Campbell stood still in shock. "I can't believe it. You challenged the power of the church. I expected you to have a polite conversation."

John Holmes nodded his head. "Campbell, I promise to call Emily. Pass a message on to her tonight. To make sure she is resting." Deep down John Holmes would make sure. Emily had some peace of mind and rest. Take good care of Buzz. After all she was a part of his life now. Finally realized. Emily was an emotional woman. Needed to be loved and cared for too. The passionate woman was dedicated to her work and life. "How many bodies so far?"

"No one has counted them yet. The dig is pain staking. What happen to your wife?"

"One day my wife was murdered. Leave it at that okay?" John Holmes was not going to allow. Campbell wasn't allowed into his personal life with Mick.

Campbell felt the sudden loss of disrespecting John Holmes had hit a wall. Wishing he had not spoken the words. The day before and yet. The flashes from the past would always be a reminder from his father's past.

The sunset on the cemetery and church streamed a golden red burst of fire. Having Buzz around was the difference of being alone. John's thoughts drifted back and forth between the cemetery and images of Emily. "Okay Campbell. Let us call it day." John assigned an officer to oversee the work left to be done. No one was expected to search around the cemetery for more bodies.

John glanced back at the cemetery as he drove away. It was difficult trying to forget it. Parked and unlocked the door punishing it open. A lonely figure felt abandoned sitting alone by the door. "Come on in Buzz glad to see you too." Emily was nowhere be found. Soothing sweet melody of her voice filled the air. A soft hummingbird like whisper soothed his thoughts. Quietly eased over to the door. Peeked around the corner. Emily rearranged the bedroom. Fresh scent of air fresher filled the air.

Emily felt a soft breeze brushing by. Buzz wagged his tail. Just to get her attention. A tall dark handsome stranger was smiling at her. Imagined how a tall swashbuckling strange man. Without any thought of being held captive. She ran over and kissed him on the lips. Held on to the stranger for dear life. John held her close staring into her dark eyes. Kissed her one more time. "Emily, I just wanted you to stay here. I think about you. Wondered whether you would be comfortable with me."

Emily kissed him again. "I hope so. Buzz and I decided to move in with you. I am lost without you. I want to be near you. John, I fell in love with you. The first day I saw you."

The crisp morning air forged a relationship for two lost souls. Emily and John discovered life together. Buzz slept at the foot of the bed. John slipped away for a shower. Emily laid still. Admiring the man and the comfort of being around him. Who chose her to be his living partner? She left him alone in the shower to prepare breakfast. Set the table and feed Buzz. Kissed John as she walked by. "Breakfast on the table. Got to shower."

Once the two arrived at the cemetery. Emily lead Buzz off to work. John Holmes surveyed the death scene. Turned around to insure the eyes of god's faith. Had assumed his perch in the window. Nothing had changed at all. John Holmes smiled. Enjoyed having the vulgar man standing above him. As the hand of god cast a long shadow of his conviction over all of them. Yet the servant of grace and compassion stood silent and still. Never faltered in his convictions of salvation and hope. It also allowed him to monitor the ongoing investigation. Being able to observe the search for the bodies of lost souls.

John sipped on the coffee. Decided to walk away from the presence of god. Inspect the graves around him for evidence. Picked up a wooden stick. Poking at the ground and searching for anything out of the ordinary. Accidently turned over some beads. A long string of beads people used inside of the church. Called up to Emily. "Please come down here with an evidence bag."

Buzz ignored John Holmes. Went about his business searching for graves. The work at hand was deemed more important. In all fairness to Buzz. It was his way of life. Buzz understood it.

Emily studied the beads. Decided to research the color and shape of the beads. Rather an odd set of beads, none of them represent the Catholic Church beads. In her opinion and cross referencing, the beads with her own set of beads. Seem like a set of homemade prayer beads. She instructed someone to bring a small hand spade. Kneeled pushing small amounts of soil. Inch by inch her hands push the soil around and away from the area of the find. Grumbling dirt clods piece by piece. The compassion pushed her fingers into the dirt. Pushing piles of dirt away from the surface dirt. Further down a piece of cloth revealed itself. Gently stroking the dirt around it. A larger piece of cloth appeared. Whistled for Buzz. Buzz galloped toward his master. Cadaver instinct sniffed around. Pushed the dirt from around the edges. A gentle stroke of pawing began to uncover a blanket covered with dirt. Buzz sat down. It was a sign. Death had found a resting place. Emily witness the compassion and respect of Buzz. Always knew when to stop and pay his respect. The rest was up to his master to finish. Buzz would sit nearby and wait for her to finish.

Emily quietly prayed over the tiny soul of a child. The beads represented his faith and hope. The fate of his outcome was a shallow grave. Tear drops replaced the pain of his death. Love from the heart of a young woman. Wiped away the child's pain in her heart.

John Holmes stood silent. Staring at an empty window. There was no one to offer a prayer over a child in a shallow grave.

Another odd occurred. Buzz had slipped away from the grave. Sniffing around a grave. Buzz pushed the dirt gently. Scratched at the edges of the dirt. Howling as he dug. Emily stood up. Franticly ran toward Buzz. It was usual for him to howl as he dug.

John Holmes ran directly toward Buzz.

Emily kneeled. Helping Buzz push away a layer of dirt. Excavating the grave became a tedious search for the unknown.

Trying to preserve the evidence. The evidence underneath the thin layer of dirt. Began to cry.

"Oh my god. It is a baby wrapped in a blanket. Take this bottle and find some milk. Hurry!" Emily lifted him up and kissed his forehead. Began to rock and sing to him.

John Holmes screamed out for a blanket. Two police officers arrived at the same time. Draped the blanket over the baby and Emily. She began to sing to him. A fresh bottle of milk was placed into his mouth. Slowly a bright-eyed little soul smiled at Emily.

John Holmes spoke out. "Start searching for evidence. I want this baby going to the hospital now! Emily take charge of him." John Holmes marched directly toward the church. Grabbed a priest. "Go tell Father Damian. To get down here now!"

The priest did not hesitate. Stumbled as he ran away from John Holmes. Screaming for help. Claiming an enraged madman had threaten his life. Trying to regain his breathe. Explaining that an insane police officer wanted Father Damian downstairs right now. A priest arrived to confront and counsel John Holmes. About his behavior and the way, he handled the young priest. "How can I be of assistance Officer Holmes?"

"Bring yourself outside. I want answers as to why. This happened outside of a cemetery." John almost grabbed the white collar. But his conscience got the better part of his actions and thoughts. "Also tell someone to bring out some warm blankets too and another bottle of warm milk."

The priest ordered the blankets and milk. "What is going on?" The two men walked outside together. John Holmes regain his composure. Explained the situation outside. The priest forgave his erratic behavior. Suggesting he would have done the same.

A young priest walked over toward the two men. Heard part of the conversation inside. Pasted both men. A calm demeanor filled with compassion and love spoke to Emily. Calmly placed a warm bottle of milk into the baby's mouth. "May I hold and feed him? I help raise seven brothers and sisters."

Emily sighed. The first miracle of life. Gave solemn compassionate young priest to her. He began to sing and feed the baby. A calmly rocked him back to sleep. Ambulance pulled up. Emily smiled. "Please you take care of him and go to the hospital with him. I will send a police car to bring you back. Oh, by the way. I did not get your name."

"I am Father James. Thank you for allowing me to care of the baby. May I call him, Robbie?"

Emily smiled and cried. "I think. That is a fitting name for him. Please stay long as you want. The officer will wait for you. When you are ready to come back. I assure you. No one will be more grateful than Robbie."

Emily stood silent, Buzz sat down by the priest and then escorted him over to the ambulance. "Buzz has a big heart too."

John whistled. "Everyone please, come in here. Take the rest of the day off. No one speak about this for now. Tomorrow I will brief you on the details. Now get out of here." John stood silent. Admired the empty grave. Smiled for a moment. Looked up at the window. The priest signed the cross. A simple peace offering for a miracle. John smiled and waved. For now. A bond of trust reached out after the unforgiving meeting.

John turned his attention to Emily. "Time to go home."

Buzz refused to leave Emily, sat outside of the shower. Waiting for Emily. John Holmes sat on the edge of the bed. Recounting the whole morning. It was as if a miracle had happened. The sound of water had stopped. Emily dried off. Observed two caring souls patiently waiting her to return. She smiled. "So much love and caring. Let me get dressed. You two go out to the kitchen and wait for dinner."

John and Buzz sighed. "Come on big boy. Mama will feed us dinner." Buzz barked at her.

Emily just laughed at them. Shut the door. Sat down on the bed. She almost wanted to cry. But decided to dress and get back to the boys outside. Open the door and Buzz ran over to her. She filled his bowl. Sat down on the floor and loved on him. John Holmes also admired her love and compassion for Buzz. Glad she found his heart and soul again. Time whispered to his thoughts. Found two loves bonding and healing his broken heart. Knew Mick would always be in his heart. Emily was a gift from heaven.

Following morning, John Holmes arrived early at the cemetery. Leaving Emily and Buzz alone. Ask her to check up on the baby. Walked about the cemetery exploring the few graves. Left open so far from the investigation. "Good morning gentleman. How are you?"

Campbell asked about Emily. "How is she doing? Is the baby doing well too?"

"I ask Emily to check up on him. How are you holding up? Also, any suspension or movement from the inside of the church?" John Holmes figured it was time to give another chance and to listen to Campbells opinion.

"John, all I ever see is the light up above. That one lone figure observing us. No one leaves the church. As if everyone inside is afraid to come out here." Campbell figured. It was best to let John Holmes speak and direct him. Safer to keep it small. To protect his self.

"Tonight, write me a report. I want to analyze it. Compare my notes to your notes." John abruptly walked away. Turned around. "Campbell go home and clean up. You look like hell warmed over too. Gentleman, please go home. I have it covered." John Holmes wanted to walk around and get some privacy. Exploring the cemetery alone would allow him to clear up his thoughts and solve some of the problems surrounding the investigation. Besides never know. When something might happen and find a better answer to any problem. Just maybe a little luck would turn over a different scenario. Marched around surveying the cemetery grounds. Trying to figure out the reason or pattern for the murders of children. Turned around to re-examine the entire area. Noticed a usual pattern surrounding the crosses. Something was different. It was out of place. A strange feeling fell over his thoughts. Something was amidst inside of the cemetery. Suddenly turned around and around. Just like a scene from the Good, Bad, and the Ugly. Realized the crosses were not all the same. But it could be from the years gone by. Still it annoyed him, why? It was a simple tombstone shaped into across. Step by step he began a walk around the line of crosses. Stopped! The cross bore no name, why? The soil was fresh under his feet. Who could have turned the soil over? Was it here all the time? Could it be a warning or answer? The obscure scene of death and crosses. Became relevant for some unknown reason. Down below the forensics team arrived. John Holmes waited inside of the arrangement of crosses. Staring directly up at the window. Observed the one person still interested in the past and the cause of death below the window. John Holmes silently admired his courage and conviction. "Okay break off into pairs. Come with me first. I will explain and show you the reason why."

Forensics crew followed. Closely picking partners to work with. John Holmes stopped by a grave marker. "One of you examine the marker. A single person walked around the grave and tombstones.

"Tell me? Did you find anything different?"

"It is rather odd. Yet will hidden too. There are new crosses here."

"The whole time we looked for a fresh grave or answers inside of this old grave site. Somehow the crosses were replaced with a new unmarked grave. I want every one of these markers re-examined inside and out." John Holmes motioned the crew to spread out. "Refer your findings to Emily. She has the day off. Save your thoughts and information for her." Turned to face the man up above standing inside of the window. Cautioned his self to be respectful. Silently thought about Father Demon up there. Wondered how long ago the man above over saw the care for the dead? Could he possibly be dreaming about life after death? Or did he want to live his life in the shoes of a fisherman. Laughed at his thoughts. Wondered if the damn fool ever knew Christ was a fisherman?

Unknown factor changed. Everyone witnesses. The usual affair between two different men. All of them hesitated to move up to the grave site. Realized it was a confrontation between two men. Being played out.

John whispered. "Yeah, I am okay for now." Pointed his finger at the window. Stood still for a long period of time. No one moved. Silence engulfed the entire dig. John finally turned around. A simple reminder folks. "No one leaves here. Until we are finished with every unmarked grave site. Make sure you label the exact grave you worked around. Emily will register each grave with a number. I want no mistakes. Do you understand me?"

The thunder of their voices roared up into the sky. "Yes sir!"

The sounds and motions of the forensic crew voices echoed off the church walls. Recreated the sound of thunder. The entire event proceeded to unearth fresh graves. Consideration was the number one protocol and respect for the dead. It all amounted to a lot of unusual amount of deaths. Where did the bodies come from? John Holmes politely walked away. Never spoke another thought.

Emily and Buzz sat patiently. Mothering Robbie. Singing and playing with him. John Holmes watch from afar. Admiring her compassion and love for unknown baby. She finally noticed

John Holmes observing her and Buzz. Motioned for him to join the love feast for Robbie's heart.

John Holmes stood still. For one moment a warm brush of air passed him by. The odd occurrence had a fresh scent of hope and love. Simply brushed it off. Smiled at the two motherly figures playing with Robbie. John Holmes smiled. A slight blush touched his face. A slight red tent covered his face. John laughed.

Emily laughed. The excitement of a grown man blushing. Assure her. She had finally found his weakness. A seven-pound baby boy stole his heart and soul.

"He giggles a lot like you too." Emily whispered. "I think he adores Buzz too." Buzz sat still wagging his tail.

A simple sigh drifted out of his mouth. For a split second. A slight schoolboy blush appeared. Emily laughed at him. As difficult as it had become. She managed to create a distraction and change his mood. "Do you think? We could give him a home and love. I think it would bring a beautiful love affair into balance. Besides Buzz needs to learn. How to babysit too."

John laughed. "When we finish here. This is completely over. Yes. Call the welfare agency to help us to do it. I think that a little happy face. Would also bring some wonderful love into my empty life. I need to learn. How to live life all over again."

Emily smiled. "Wait till you get home." Emily kissed Robbie on the cheek. Robbie giggled. John Holmes pulled her away. Away to kiss her. But a bundle of giggles stopped that kiss. Emily was still holding Robbie. All of them laughed. John Holmes finally found peace of mind and hope. His thoughts returned to last moments of the day. Emily found her freedom. John Holmes spent a few hours with a thirteen-year-old girl and a dog. All three of them sat on the porch together. Watched pull her leave that day. Never expecting to see her again. But this time it was a blessing. Life gave her second chance to finish her failure. The day she ran away from home. A quiet evening alone with John and Buzz. Buzz found a place on the bed and curled up. The threesome drifted off to sleep.

"Time to go back to work." Emily woke up the late sleepers. John Holmes cracked one eye. Buzz rolled belly up. "Get up sleepy heads or no breakfast."

John Holmes rolled over pushing Buzz off the bed. Buzz growled and jumped on top of him. John wrestled him to the floor. Buzz barked at him. Ran away to the kitchen. It was time to eat. Barking at Emily. Sat down patiently for his bowl. Emily slide a plate of eggs and bacon to him. Buzz finished off the plate. Walked to the door and barked. Emily let him out to do his business. A few minutes later Buzz sat at the door. Emily open the door. John sat down and the mooch sat down next to him. John finished eating. "Not today big boy. Time you earned your keep today. Open the drawer of treats. Hid the treats in his pocket for Buzz. Emily walked over and kissed him.

"Ready to go to work?"

"Guess I should appear before the court of life and heaven."

"John, time to go. Until we finish this crime. Find the answers for a reason and why. It will haunt all of us forever."

"I know. But why did all this happen over such a long time. Does Mary Jane Hudson fit into this crime somewhere?"

"John, no one has an answer to the past yet. But if the two are tied together. Then maybe we can close this case."

"Yea, you could be right. But why so many kids? How long has this been going on? No one seems concerned?"

"Because someone has a reason to cover it up. We have a reason to find out. Time to go to work."

No matter what. There was a reason for all of this. John Holmes was determined to find that one reason. This morning the only link between heaven and hell. Were the lost lives of children from the past and the present? John Holmes stood still. The cemetery had tried to bury the past. Only to open the door into the present. He walked around the area. Trying to piece the path and reasons for the crosses. John Holmes studied the section over and over. A simple reason for what? Created a barrier between life and death. What reason would a molester have to rape and murder children? Where did the children come from now? A place where their lives and names had no meanings. If the children were orphans. Who provided a way to use them for a price? A child's life was worth nothing. Why? Who would coverup the accidental death of a child being molested for a profit? There was grace or hope for an abused child. John Holmes stood alone. Observing the one man. Who observed his work? Offering nothing in exchange for the reasons or the truth. Sadly, John Holmes felt compelled to express his anger. In the silence of his thoughts. Stood still listen to the sound of life around him. Paused a moment to search for an answer. Up above a man of god still. Observing one man. John

Holmes stared directly into soul. Raised on arm and saluted him. Raised one arm and saluted him one finger. Held high above his head. Rebellion often cures the heart of a lot of miserable people.

The soft ground underneath his feet. Began trembled his legs almost gave way. The landscape used to bury a person of good conscience. Cast a darker image of death. Forensics began to uncover more bodies. The crossing patten in the cemetery. Exposed a long-lost dark secret. That was buried in the vaults of time. The body count rose day after day. The timeline of the past and present ran side by side. The strange crosses were markers not grave sites. John Holmes hollered Campbell and Emily to come up to the hilltop.

Waved to police officer guarding the grave sites. "Take Campbell, somewhere to buy some shoes or boots." Emily laughed at John Holmes and Campbell. "I want the dirt not his shoes. But I also need to examine the bottom of the shoes."

Emily picked up the pair of shoes. Flipped them over and over. Placed the shoes into a plastic bag and tagged them. Began to take soil samples of the dirt around the graves. Walked away from the cemetery. Toward the outside church walls. Began examining the soil around the plants and trees. Kneeled scraping up soil samples from the trees and plants. Somewhere in the area of the church grounds. Soil was being removed used to bury the bodies. Where was the recreation room of death? The boy's bodies had to be murdered and abused within the walls of the sanctuary. She had another thought. It occurred within her on thoughts. What if the school and orphan boys were connected? It would be a recreational paradise for religious perverts in god's paradise. Emily whistles for Buzz. His head perked up. Ran down toward his master. Sat down beside of her waiting for a command. She placed the shoe in front of Buzz. Buzz carefully examined the shoe. A strange odd occurrence took her breath away. Buzz stood still and sat down on the ground by the tree. She stopped. Decided to examine the soil. Emily whistled at John Holmes to come down.

John Holmes witnessed the strange occurrence. Why was Buzz sitting on the ground in front of the building in front of a tree? John walked around it. Before he motioned for help. A crew to came down.

"I know. Just be patient. Stand back for a change. Let this take care of itself. Buzz come here." Buzz walked away and sat down by his master. She hugged him. The definition of death lingered into hours and hours. Waiting proved to be a villain within her thoughts. It created a depression and lack of reasoning for just sitting there. Emily stood up and motioned Buzz to stand. Decided to examine the bags of evidence. One by one she began to sort it out. Writing notes on the bags content. Nothing appeased her thoughts. A great deal of sadness covered her thoughts. Through all the searches. Trying to analyze it. Just for a tiny bit of clues or identities. Hoping to figure out the time and ages of the deaths.

Buzz wandered off alone. The dog's instinct began to focus on another area. No one paid any attention to the K-9 detective. Except one detective. John Holmes admired the instinct that lead Buzz in search of the past. Slipping away from the investigation, followed Buzz. Buzz took no concern or notice. John Holmes politely followed him. The scent of death produced the same instinct of death within a minute. The k-9 began to search a clump of dead flowers and brushes. Buzz did not sit down. Began to dig into the ground. John Holmes wondered if he was searching for food or water. After ten minutes of digging and sniffing. Buzz stopped and sat down. John Holmes walked over gave him a treat. He managed to carry it around for Buzz. Kneeling and pushing the dirt out of the dig. Sudden shock forced him to fall back. The last thing anyone would have suspected. Proved to be a complete surprise. John Holmes held his breath and nose. The odor was over whelming. A face of a full-grown man appeared. "How did you get here?"

Emily searched for Buzz and John Holmes. Stopped in her footsteps. Foul odor drifted toward her senses. Turned around searching for her equipment. John Holmes had kneeled to puke from the odor. Buzz stayed true to his work and cause. Did not move.

Emily called someone on her cell phone. Ask for her and equipment. Wanted help to remove a body from the ground. Quickly outpaced her thoughts to rescue John Holmes and Buzz. Shoved a mask into his hands. Pulled Buzz away from the sickening smell of death and rot. "Come on you two get back. I need room to operate and figure out this mess. Hope I can identify the body."

John Holmes and Buzz stepped back. Realized that Emily was about invoke her privilege of being a forensic expert. John Holmes admired her courage for being able to get past the scent and smell of rotting corpse. A pail disgusting rotting face offered an unwarranted picture of death. John realized Buzz moved away from him. Decided to sit down beside his master to protect her from anyone. Buzz understood the woman's temperament and work ethic. John Holmes suddenly learned a lot about the young woman in his life. She was a professional at work.

John Holmes motioned for everyone assisting Emily to comply with her orders. Do their utmost to achieve and assist her with anything. The unwanted stench of a rotting corpse. Left everyone wanting fresh air. She calmly went about her business. Silently walking away back up toward the other dig. First, she walked back to his car. Opened the door and sat down to collect her thoughts. It was a silent reminder of her life. The past offered little reminders of death. How Christopher Robin lived a double life. The reality of facing a greater threat. That someone out there covered up more than one murder. But the lifetime of abuse and death of children was totally unacceptable. After collecting her thoughts. Stepped out of the drivers sit. Walked back up the hill. Stood silent staring and praying for an answer. Turned to look up and stare at the same window. As John Holmes had constantly did. It was an empty window. Wondered why all the interest at first?

John Holmes intervene. Studied the empty window. Such an empty place under the shadow of darkness. Was the church really involved in this crime? Or was there another motive into the deaths to protect someone outside of the church. Who was the dead man? Why was he buried there? Everything was a collection of thoughts. Empty stood silent. Together they walked back up to the unmarked graves.

A collection of lost souls from the grave were begging for help. John Holmes ignored the cries. All he wanted was a simple answer. Sadly, it amounted to thirty graves and one little baby boy. A tear rolled over the lower part of his eyes. Moisture continued roll downward. Passed over the top part of his upper lip. A moist drop of passion of life. Touched his heart. An everlasting sense of failure turned into hope. The symbolic compassion touched his thoughts. It reminded him of life before and after the loss of his wife. The courage of child and her dog. Quietly waiting for someone. Who would help them to get home? Realized every child behind him was waiting to go home too.

Emily stood up. Silence engulfed her thoughts. She finished her search. Bagged the evidence and packed it away to be analyzed. Stood silent. Wondered about the days and nights in the cemetery. Where did it all go wrong? Who started the sexual abuse of children? Why did a little angel appear? A brutal crime against children. So far no one on God's green earth was under arrest. Closed her eyes to cover the sins. In all things evil, there was no proof of anyone committing a crime, why? Somewhere in all the evidence. There was a criminal to be found.

Time to collect her thoughts and consider it a day. She needed a fresh start to examine the body. But the haunting experience into the faces of death were children and one full grown dead man. She studied the area. Why would someone bury a dead man near the church? Obviously, it was to cover up the crime. The odd sense of reality was the unmarked graves. Was it an angel trying to provide the truth and a convicted killer? A silent voice was trying to expose the truth. Whoever chose? How to expose the truth was not a criminal. Where were the children coming from? Who did the hideous crimes of death? How long has this been going on? When did the earlier deaths occur? Also, the strange reoccurrence of fresh bodies. Suddenly realized there was no sign of John Holmes. She swiftly turned her head found Him. Standing alone. Realized he was focusing and trying to solve a crime. Patted her leg for Buzz to come. The two of them walked up the hill. Came face to face with the man. A dark grimace of pain and thoughts on his face. "John, stop. Time to go home. This is not a reason to make it personal. Come on leave it here." She touched his hand and held it. Began to pull him back into the real world.

John stood still and smiled. "Sorry. I was into a deep thought. You are right. Time to go home. I need a shower. I am covered with the stench of death. Buzz my man. You need bath too. You smell. You need to drop him off at a groomer."

Emily laughed at John. "Only mama bathes her baby boy. I will take him with me. Meet you at home." Emily blew him a kiss. Buzz barked at him and sat down. John pulled a treat out of his pocket. Feed Buzz. That was the end of that conversation. Buzz ran away to be with Emily.

"Damn dog. Buzz you are a moocher." John Holmes laughed. "Buzz is the king of exposing a crime. I am glad you are my buddy."

A familiar voice split the air. "Quite the dog. John, we are lucky to have those two. What is the next thing to do?" Campbell suspected the two of them of being together. Being close to enough to be romantic lovers too.

John Holmes noticed the sarcasm in his tone. Decided to ignore the comment. "Come with me." John Holmes walked him to a place beside by the church. "Use the night crew to search this area one more time. I want a complete check of it. We found a body of a man here today. Do we understand each other?"

Campbell listened to the insult. Follow by a stern warning from John Holmes. Who tolerated nothing concerning his life? Next time he would choose his words carefully. Wishing he should have not mentioned the subject. John Holmes was not a forgiving man to work for.

"We will walk it together. It may be easier for you to understand. I was a little harsh on you. If you check around all the unmarked graves. You will notice the soil samples are mixed with the soil already here. The body was also covered with it. Emily found the sample of soil on your shoes. It was used to bury the man. Mixed in with the other soil. So, someone came here to rid their selves of a body. Sometime tonight leave here early. Report back in the morning here. You and I are going hunting inside the church and outside of it. I will call a judge to get a search warrant. Got it?"

"Sure, John. Take care of yourself. Get a goodnights rest."

Campbell realized being disrespectful. Mixing his sarcasm was not acceptable. Plus, John's life was none of his business or thoughts. But he would save that for another day.

John Holmes just walked away. Leaving Campbell to figure out the rest. A beautiful woman with a dog. Proved to be a better night. Thinking about the scent of her body and love. Loomed over his unforgiving encounter with Campbell. John left the far away site of the church and cemetery. Thought about Emily. The scent of her hair and admiring her smile. A simple evening of just sitting there alone with her. Almost to surreal to be true. Opening the front door proved to be a disturbing moment. There was a large fur ball blockade. Buzz sat down in front of him and refused to move. "Emily, please bring Buzz a treat. I am under house arrest. He refuses to move."

Emily appeared smiling. Wearing a see-through teddy. Pitched a treat at Buzz. He quickly forgot about John. John stuttered trying to express his thanks. "What is for dinner?"

"Fried chicken, mash potatoes, green beans, and hot rolls in the bed." Emily smiled. John Holmes blushed an ultra-violent red. Buzz would not of this charade and step between them. Emily dropped him another treat. Pressed her lips to his lips. She took away his breath. "Time for dinner and a treat later, my love."

John Holmes smiled. But the sensual thought of her being an exotic treat. Created a new problem, the scent of dirt and sweat forced him to shower. Leaving the desert for later. The three-course dinner delight. Danced around a candle lit evening. Sensual night hours lifted the spirits of love. Buzz ignored the playful romp of two lovers. Only the musical sound being played a golden retriever could be heard.

SHADOW OF DEATH

Death is an unwarranted compassion of life. Brings only sorrow and pain into the realm of life and hope. Leaving empty souls. Lifeless figures frozen in time. A vacuum of life filled with empty souls staring blindly into the darkness. The shadows the past hover over a person unable to say good-bye. No one can hear or understand. Why it is an empty garden of death.

Sun light dawned and it came with a simple kiss. The sun light would share a darker side. All the forgotten faces suspended in some-where in time. Laying between under piles of dirt or on cold steel slabs. The odyssey of death was suspended between heaven and hell. One by one the dying sound of voices began to pry open the door of silence.

Emily cast her hopes and evidence on the forgotten victims passing between life and death. Bodies covered beneath white sheets on a cold slab of steal.

She wished once more to be a child again. Hoping her last life experience would have never happen. But those thoughts faded away. The present-day life gave back her a passion to be alive and thankful for surviving her experience of living with a serial killer. Emily walked and studied the bodies surrounding her on the stainless-steel slabs. One by one she would search for evidence and cause of death. It would at least share a beginning leading back into the past. The frozen expressions on their faces begged for answers. The tearful face of the lady searching for answers. Proved to be her strength. It was proved to be enough determination. To solve and convict the injustice of life itself. Created by those who prey upon a child? Whose perversion and fantasies found pleasure assaulting a child. She never noticed John Holmes walked in on her.

John Holmes stood silent. Studied her passion. As she was trying to solve a crime and fill in the blanks. Placed a cup of coffee on her table. Emily turned and smiled. "Thank you." Returned to her work.

"Please forgive my intrusion. But I am going to invade the church. Can you help me? With some type of theory or answers."

"John, this is so disgusting. This child was physically abused. The buttocks have penetration wounds. Notice the bruises on the arms. Someone held him down. Approximate age is around ten. The victim was strangled. Probably some kind of an accident to prevent him from screaming. Needless to say. I want to scream." She broke down and cried. John held on to her for dear life. Buzz stood silent.

"Emily, come outside. Take some time to gather yourself. I know you feel their pain. But one by one we will solve this crime. Come on Emily and bring Buzz. He seems a bit hurt seeing you cry."

Emily bent over and kissed his nose. "Come on big fella. You and mama need's fresh air." Turned around and kissed John. "Thank you, my love." Together the three of them walked away. Outside into the open air.

John stood still. Never moved for a moment. Felt an unknown presence. Somewhere around the outside area. "Emily act normal. Someone is watching us." John Holmes walked further out on to the parking lot. Instinct proved to be right. A priest stood behind a tree. Observing the two of them. "Please step out into the open. If you have any questions? I suggest you come forward. I am a police officer."

For a few moments he stood still. Before walking out into the open parking lot. Lifted his hands up into the air. To insure his on safety. "I am sorry. I did not mean to startle you. May I put my hands down please?"

John Holmes almost laughed at the meekness of a young youthful priest. "Oh, hell, come over here."

It was an awkward situation at first. But the young priest relaxed. His fear soon disappeared. "Again, I am sorry."

Emili almost laughed at the timid young priest. "I am sure. This is more than a chance meeting. Why are you here?"

John Holmes shrugged his shoulder. As if to say oh well. Please continue.

"I am here of my own choice. But I do not want it to reflect upon my life. I gave up my mortal life to serve God. But my faith is wavering right now. I watched you. Yesterday under the trees and on the hill. I am saddened by the sight. I have seen. But a crime has been committed. It was not the church. By a certain group of men. Who have created this obscene crisis?"

John Holmes unfolded his arms. Stood silent. Emily reacted. To his emotional stance. "John, what now?"

"I have a strange feeling. That whatever is coming. Will offend a lot of people. Create a lot of self-denial of the crime. But I will need to sit down with this priest." Emily decided to question the priest.

"Wait. I want to talk with him first."

"Go ahead."

"What is your name?"

"I am James Winston. I am a novice in the church. I am studying the priest hood."

"How old are you, James?"

"I am twenty years old."

John Holmes was amazed at her intuition. She simply applied a basic conversation. To seduce his weakness and thoughts.

"I am sorry, my name is Emily." She quickly shook his hand. Gaining his confidence to relax and speak with her. "You are quite a young man. Wanting to be a part of the church and give your life to Christ. What made you want to do this?"

"I wanted to be a priest sense my childhood. I enjoyed doing Sunday services. After high school I applied to be one."

"Good for you. What made you decide to talk with us?"

"It is important to do the will of god. The priest hood is about giving and sharing your life. To do good deeds for all of god's children."

"That is a wonderful attribute to have James. Can I ask you one more question?"

"Sure, go ahead."

"Do you know who did this? Are you willing to share some answers?"

"I cannot say for sure. But at night in my room. I can hear the screams of children. It carries through the vents. I always see a group of men leave at night." James Winston humbled his self before Emily.

"Where do the children come from?"

"From a window above. I see cars come and go. But the sadness is watching children come and go."

"Do you know from where?"

"No, I do not know that. I only feel the shame and sadness of my failure to stop it."

Emily thanked him. "James thank you. For now, please tell no one about our conversation. You may leave now." Emily turned to John Holmes and shook her head. Back and forth as to say. Do not intervene. John Holmes stood silent and shocked. Two of them watched as he drove away.

"Well that was a great conversation. Why did you let him go?"

"Because it is basic crime solving. Let him continue to witness the crime. Because you need an airtight case to arrest anyone. I am sorry. But the obscene sickness will continue until. We can protect those children. I got a plate number. I turned him around to see. Where he was going."

John kissed her. "You are quite a detective."

Emily laughed at him. But she also played well at getting information. "I wonder. How deep and where this case is going now? I still want to figure out the timeline. From the time it started until today so far. I cannot help but wonder. Who is involved in this massive act of being a child predator? What if this is a ring of pedophiles?"

John Holmes felt the sadness. Disturbed by the actions of grown adults. Perversion terrorizing young children for sexual behavior and being a ring of pedophiles. "God help us if this deeper than a normal ring of pedophiles. But one thing will happen. A lot of sickos will be behind bars."

"John, what if this is a simple hidden group of pedophiles? Who use young children for pleasure? I mean a local group within this town." Emily feared the worst. A small group of men being pedophiles. The face of death was started long before she was born.

John saw and felt the tears forming and rolling out over her eyes. A single finger caught them one by one. He held them in his palm. "Don't worry. I promise. I will protect you."

Emily touched his heart. "I know. You will. Come on back inside and review the evidence from the first victim. At least we can identify the cause and time of death."

"Tell me about this man."

"Considered a lot older than most men. Probably in his seventies, found contusions and bruises to the temple. I doubt. He could have sex. There is a slight problem. The sack is empty. For some reason he was castrated. Considering the age and scarring around the lower extremities of the lower body. Someone butchered his sexual drive. Maybe he was gay too. If the church goers found out. Or if he was found out. Someone decided to fix him. That would keep him silent for the rest of his life. The other side of life is revenge. Revenge is a deadly thought to consider in the end. Maybe it was time to wish upon his enemies. I found this on his body. It was inside of his suit coat. A small handgun probably to protect his self but revenge came with a death wish too."

"So, we can add murder to the list. Problem is. I have never seen him around town." John Holmes considered it. To be a rather odd sort of thing to try and understand.

"Which brings us back to Jack Winston. Why was he here? What was he searching for?" Emily in her thoughts tried to piece it all together. But the unknown factor was no identity for the victim.

"I think tomorrow. I will ask Campbell about him. I will ask him to come by and try to identify the victim. Are you two ready go home?" John flipped Buzz a treat.

"Come on Buzz. Daddy is ready to go home. I am tired too. Been a long and rather odd day." Emily kissed Buzz. "Don't worry. You will yours later." The evening was set a quiet evening of being alone. No one to bother them. The night drifted quietly into the night.

Early morning alarm changed the silence. Buzz snapped from a somber silent night. Rough and ready for breakfast. John slipped away to shower. Emily prepared breakfast. John Holmes ate and kissed her good-bye. Emily stared down at Buzz. Smiled at him. Walked away to get dressed. Drove back to the morgue. Stood still alone in an empty chamber of death and victims. Buzz curled up in his bed. Studying Emily's emotions. Buzz never slept. As long there was work, to be done.

Studying the world of being a criminal also would take another turn. Emily researched the files and fingerprints of the victim from the day before. The file from the F.B.I. revealed quite a surprise. Dead man was in the witness protection program. Well known pedophile. Who testified against a priest?

Who was at one time the archbishop of the city of New York? Moved here twenty years ago. The odd factor in the whole story was a surprise. It was Maxwell Van Der Berg. The informant was well known pedophile in the circle of child molesters. Emily read every page of his known activities of the underground world of pedophiles. From selling young girls to be sex slaves, molesting school age children under ten years of age. The most surprising factor was his new name, Jackson Winston Senior. Called John to come to her office.

John arrived about twenty minutes later. "What's up?" Dropped a treat to the floor for Buzz.

"Come into my office. Need a little privacy." Emily and John walked side by side. As if nothing had happened from the phone call. John Holmes understood the language. Decided the thought should be held in a secure area inside of a closed office. To hear Emily's implications and story. After the information was shared. Emily reminded him about Jack Winston. "I think you need to pick him up. There are a few missing pages to his story. That need to be filled in by our junior priest. If that is the truth?"

"Well I am glad. You decided to let him go. It must be his grandfather. I am sure. That the old man may have raped him too. But first assume he is innocent for now." John sat silent and dialed the phone.

Campbell answered. "What ups John?"

"Meet me at the church."

"Be right there in a few minutes." Campbell arrived before John Holmes. Stood outside in the sunshine. Observing the dig at the cemetery. Felt a lot of remorse thinking about all the deaths surrounded by a lot of mystery and disgrace.

John Holmes decided to stop at the door. Quietly motioned Campbell to come over. "We are going to walk around the church. Searching for someone. I do not want to raise any suspicion for now. I will let you know. If I see this person. Do not do anything at all."

Campbell nodded. Never ask any questions. For better or worse it and it was an order.

John Holmes opened the door to the cathedral. Admired the artwork on the walls. Fresh scent of candles burning inside. Never once did he kneel. The echo footsteps echoed off the walls. The perfect entrance into a sanctuary of redemption. The life and death before the image Jesus Christ. Provided an opening conversation of death outside the holy eternal doors to heaven and forgiveness. Wooden oak doors began to creak as the hands of justice pushed them open. A young priest stepped forward. John smiled at him. "Good day Jack?"

"How are you, Mister Holmes?" Jack politely spoke. Never once did he suspect. John Holmes was about to question him.

"I need a few minutes of your time. I hope. We can clear up this matter."

"Please tell me. What you need." Jack openly agreed to answer the questions.

"Do you know Jackson Winston? He is the dead man. We found yesterday. Could you possibly identify him? If you know him. John Holmes used a pleasant tone to avoid a conflict.

"I was afraid to ask you questions about my uncle. I caught a glimpse of his body. I am sure you know about his background. He was a mob informant. Also, a pervert in sheep's clothing. After being caught with a child. You saw the outcome of that. I am sure. Anything else?" Jack hoped for forgiveness and reassurance. Hoping the forth coming information would set him free.

"Thank you for your time. I am glad. You cleared up this matter for me." John Holmes shook his hand. Walked away from the conversation. Whispered to Campbell. "He is lying though his teeth."

"How do you know."

"A lair never makes direct eye contact. He focused his attention directly at the floor. Did not make direct eye contact." John Holmes searched for slicked things created by fear. It would expose any natural weakness or character flaw of the human soul.

Campbell could do little to stop the intimidation created by John Holmes. John Holmes purposely used that tactic.

John Holmes would conjure up the many faces and weakness of any human being. Yet he saw the world in the different way. One filled with kindness and hope toward people. Who seem to suffer the pains and sorrow of life inside of their hearts? Hoping someone would share the truth? "Campbell, give me your thoughts on this investigation?"

Campbell stopped in his tracks. A bit shaken by the question. "John, faith in God is one thing. The facts are sorted out piece by piece. But the thought of someone molesting children. Is sick. Do you think the children buried in the unmark graves were molested?"

"All I have are their bodies. Mostly skeleton bones. I am unable to identify them. Yet the most recent ones. Scare the living hell out of me. How do you look into their eyes? It is as if that child was begging for help. The silence is the damnation of failure me and you too. Is this part of the damnation your father left behind inside that damn file too? How do I face the reality of this crime? By discovering the damn truth. Right now. Emily is doing the forensic work. She will write a file of discovery. With a full detailed report of her findings."

That painful encounter with Jack Winston. Only answered a few questions.

"John, what do you expect from me. I cannot change the things in my father's life."

"I didn't ask you too. I expect you to tell me the truth. So far that seems far and between. I do not have an answer for his past. But you must tell the truth. If you want an answer to his past and yours."

"What if I am afraid of the truth?"

"Then you better find the answer. I cannot solve your past or this crime without you doing your job and telling me the truth." John Holmes lacked any type of remorse. Every question into his past and father's past. "Why?"

"I am sure if of a lot of things. Some may affect my life. I am sure if it will save me from the past and the present."

"Campbell, you have two choices. One is to walk away. The other is to face your past and clear up the lives of every child buried in the cemetery."

John Holmes turned around. Stood silent for a few seconds. "I suggest. You and god find a way to solve your past and guilt. Come back to see me. When you have made a decision about your life." Walked away.

Campbell stood alone on the edge of life. For once in his life. Forced to confront the demons from his past. No one around to lean on or direct him. Or help him with the task before him.

John Holmes never turned back. Decided to let Campbell suffer alone. Hoping Campbell would resolve the conflict inside of him.

After talking with Jack Winston. John Holmes never realized. He was walking inside of the crosses. Sound of silence engulfed him in darkness. One by one. Walking and searching for answers. The only question of thought why? Why would so many children die alone? Why would a grown man molest the pure innocence of a child? Yet one single child was given a dream and hope. After tethering on the break of death. The symbol of life was a little boy. The child was blessed by the compassion of one priest. Who feed and named him? John Holmes realized. The heart ache and pain in his life was not a curse. It was the compassion from two women. Guiding him through the sorrows and failures of his life. John Holmes stood still. The cemetery consisted of forgotten children. There was no time to accept failure and lose hope. Decide to invoke one more action. Turned his attention to the window above the cemetery.

Politely saluted the man in the window. One single digit stood erect. John Holmes bowed before walking away. Shouted out loud for the world to hear. "What we have here. Is a failure to communicate."

Sound of silence was left far behind. John Holmes drove away. Never looked back at the cemetery. Long for a place called home. The scent of a woman and moocher for a snack. The scent of a woman drifted in and out of his thoughts. Pushed the door open. Walked inside of the apartment. Aroma of fresh cooked meal drifted into his sense of smell. Heard a humming musical sound. Emily never noticed or heard him enter. Buzz politely sat down. Waited for a treat. John wagged his finger back and forth. Denying Buzz, a treat. Placed his finger on his mouth. As if Buzz would understand to be quiet. Walked over and kissed her neck. Emily ignored the moisture of his kiss. "You smell like Buzz today. I suggest you shower before dinner. Get along little man. I expect a well groom lover to come back for dinner."

John Holmes fell victim to the same thing. He complained about with Buzz. The scent of a foul odor of failure. Claimed its next victim. One John Holmes. Emily heard the shower running. Bellowing sounds of a cow singing in the rain of a shower head. She laughed. Buzz howled.

A dark stranger reappeared. Whistled at the youthful young lady. Preparing his dinner before stealing a kiss. Emily pushed him away toward the table. "If you do not obey me. There will be no treat after dinner. Do you understand me?"

A sigh filled the air. A child like fool. Hung his head down. "Okay." Grabbed Emily. Kissed her lips and laughed. "Don't worry. I am sitting down."

"Damn kids are all alike." Placed a late on the floor for Buzz. "Thought you would be served first. Didn't you?"

"Well I kind of knew. I was playing second fiddle to the four-legged prince."

"John, you never quit. The slick little charmer. But you know what? I love. Sense of humor little man." Emily walked over and kissed him.

The enchanted evening was a simple moment of life. The two lovers found solace within each other's arms. The lengthy day had cast a long shadow. A reminder that life also moved forward. Tragedy did not linger far behind the search for the truth. A full moon was replaced by glowing sunlight coming through the curtains. The alarm began to reset back to the day before. John rolled over only the other side was empty. Emily was nowhere to be found. Buzz was gone too. Walked out into the kitchen. Found a note on the refrigerator. (Sorry John, but I discovered another possible answer. Hoping my work will lead us to an answer. Love Emily.)

John dressed. Walked away from the apartment. Wondering what Emily had on her mind. John Holmes called Campbell. "Forget the report and meet at the morgue." Hung up on Campbell. Campbell felt a shock wave. Empty emotional state of confusion. John Holmes called and hung up on him. The sound of his voice was a calm demeanor. But the urge to run over held a grip on his senses. It was not a time to panic. It was a time to follow orders. Campbell decided to leave and follow his orders without any hesitation.

John Holmes found Emily's car at the morgue. A sigh of relief and confusion happed at the same time. Why did she leave without a word? John opened the door. Stood silent. Never spoke a word. Emily stood still. Held her breathe and blew out. Whispering to Buzz. "Some way Buzz. I must find a reason and why? All these kids died a painful death. Who would want to do terrible things to them? Somewhere in this room. There is a reason for this. Must be a clue in here. Little Robbie is depending on us too." A long sigh drifted into the air. She wiped away a tear.

"Don't worry. We will find and answer. Trust me. Please do not ever scare the hell out of me again."

"I should have known. There is nowhere to hide from you. Thank you." Emily held her emotions. Was afraid that someone would find out. She preferred to keep it to herself.

Campbell rushed inside. Fearing the worst possible scenario. "Is everything okay?"

John Holmes turned around. "Yeah. It was a false alarm. Nothing to worry about Campbell. I am sorry. Never meant to scare you."

"That is okay. It would not be the same without Emily and Buzz." Campbell blushed.

"I came to work early this morning. Never reported in and John was worried about me. So, he panicked. Started searching for me and Buzz. Found us here at work."

Campbell smiled. "Good thing. He is concerned about you and the rest of us."

Emily seemed to enjoy the lie. Keeping Campbell at bay. "So, while you two are here. There are a few odd traces of chemicals in Jackson Winston blood sample. Also, a bit of poison in his stomach area. Someone must have wanted him shut up."

Campbell spoke promptly. "It would seem likely. I am guessing here. Someone was about to be outed. Just my thought."

"That is a good point. Next problem. Trying to find a source. Who could validate it?"

"John, the closest source of information. Is our young priest. I suggest a visit. I will try to find a source and cause of death."

John Holmes acknowledge Emily. "We have a few options. But Winston will be the first. Until you find a few more answers. Check back later."

"Hope you two find a few answers." Emily kept her private thoughts to herself. Buzz ignored the whole conversation.

"Campbell meet me at the church." John Holmes walked him to the door. Stood still and watched Campbell leave. Walked back inside to see Emily. "Next you sneak out. Tell me. I was worried about you two. I came here. To insure you were safe."

"John, you have had a few rough days. Figured you needed to sleep longer. Stop worrying. I am safe with my bodyguard. Besides. I know better. You know. I do not take chances. Besides. I love you and Buzz." Emily kissed him. Shoved him out the door.

John Holmes parked outside of the church. Stood still admiring the dark empty shadow in the window above the cemetery. Wondered where the priest was? Realized it was just an empty thought. Campbell approach him.

"What now?"

John Holmes pushed his shoe back and forth. Silently thinking about the inside of the church. How to go about confronting Jack Winston. Decided on a bit of tact and compassion. Hoping to lure him in a comfortable zone. "Well Campbell. Guess our faith and fate are destined to meet inside." Walked away. Heading straight for the doors.

Campbell noticed a sense of compassion. It was almost if he whispered to him. Never spoke a word. Waiting for the encounter inside of the church.

John Holmes stopped a young priest. "Could you please ask Jack Winston to come and speak with me?"

The young priest offered to lead the two police officers to him. Sound of silence echoed off the marble floor. Young priest opened the doors to the chapel. Jack Winston was kneeling and praying. No one spoke or interfered with his confessions before God. John Holmes and Campbell sat down in the back row. Campbell kneeled and prayed. Jack Winston finished his prayers, Stood. Turned to face the two police officers. Calmly walked to the back of the church. Offered a way to leave and go outside of the church. Guided the men into garden of flowers and trees. Sanctuary away from all the noise and motion inside. Offered a bench to sit down on. The moral fiber of life was in the garden of

Eden. Set to cast an apple upon the face of reality. With exception of having a woman to bite into the apple of fate.

John Holmes tempted Jack Winston with an open hand of reassurance. The moment of the handshake. Shifted the conversation instantly. "Jack, I want the truth about your uncle. I am tired of finding to many children. In the cemetery outside of this church and your uncle's dead body."

Campbell sat silent and stunned.

Jack Winston trembled. Almost lost the will to breathe. "I dreaded this moment. I was sure it would come sooner or later." Twisted the rosery around a fist.

Campbell tried to ease his conscience. "Jack, this isn't about you. We need more information concerning your uncle."

John Holmes softly spoke. "I am not her to convict you. But I need your help. Your uncle is dead. Why?"

A tearful child appeared. Trembling with a hand full of beads. "I lived in shame. My uncle molested me. Threated me. If I spoke out. Sometimes I would attend the parties. No one touched me. But the horror of seeing children. Offered as sex slaves to men was disgusting." Jack Winston broke down and cried.

John Holmes swallowed his thoughts. But the one thing in his mind. Never faded away. Being a police officer required strength and character. Self-pity was not acceptable. "Jack, I feel your pain. But sympathy is not in play. Every child out there and in the morgue is not acceptable." Silence shifted the way. Everything was going to unfold.

Campbell held his thoughts and breath. Saw the power of a reckoning. Having to face a man. Who no longer would except his on failure?

James Winston failed the moment of truth. The tears of fear and shame were no longer an excuse to hide. The pain and suffering of his past.

"I want all the facts and truth about your deceased uncle. From the beginning till his death." John Holmes dropped the gloves. Unfortunately, during the moment of truth. A voice intervened on his part.

"Detective Holmes, have you no shame? His silence is protected by the church. I suggest you get a warrant. Come James. Time to confess your sins." Reached down and lifted Jack Winston up. Dark side of God's sins was the back of a black jacket.

John Holmes held his thoughts. Motion Campbell to follow him. The two men walked back into the church. Walked into the sun light.

"Campbell, our first encounter was a positive moment. I got one thing out of it. A confession from the church."

"You did all this to get a reaction. From the priest in charge?"

"The virtue of temptation is the first sin. The second sin is the truth. Third James Winston knows more than that. The church is hiding the truth."

Campbell tried to understand John Holmes. None of it made sense. But then again John Holmes was not exactly a man to fail. "So, you came here. To force a conflict with the head of the church."

"Not exactly. I wanted Jack Winston more than the church. His dead uncle is the key to the truth. To the past and the present-day deaths. But now the church has confessed to a sin. I hope it will reveal the answers." John Holmes played his hand. Never expected the encounter. Leaving him with a far greater challenge. "Campbell, do me a favor. Come back here later tonight. Walk up to the cemetery. Let no one know you are here. Watch the back door to the chapel. I want a list of the coming and going. Get some night vision to do it. Wear dark clothes too."

Campbell almost smiled. Thing about being a spy. The cloak and dagger scenario would be exciting. "Okay John. Anything else?"

"No. Stay out of sight and mind. I do not want anyone to know you are here."

John Holmes simply walked away. Leaving Campbell alone with his thoughts and mission. John Holmes was about to return to the morgue. Spend time with Emily and Buzz. Listen to her crime report too.

Emily's thoughts reoccurred about her youthful past. It was about who held her captive? Proved to be blessing in her life. She never forgot his passion to reward her for her kindness and love. The last dying days of his life was the greatest moment his life. Christopher Robin found peace, compassion, and forgiveness from a thirteen-year-old girl and a rowdy loveable dog. Buddy was the love her life. He never left her side. But all things must pass too. But memories were forever within her heart and soul. Looked at Buzz. "You know your daddy was quite character Buzz. I miss him."

John quietly listened to her thoughts. Also felt her pain and loss. Seeing a thirteen-year-old child sitting side by side with Buddy. Standing still watching the two of them drive away. Whispered to his self. "I miss him too."

Emily heard the whisper too. "I guess Buddy. Is here to relieve the pain of life. Sharing his love with us along with Buzz." Emily gave Buzz a treat. "You are a good boy too."

"Spent part of the morning with Jack Winston. Before the head priest shut us down. Forbid him from talking to us."

Emily stood silent. "John, I have been over this man's death. Someone took his life. The problem is a matter of where and when. The site of discovery is not the site of his murder."

"Maybe the only witness with answers is Jack Winston. How do we lure him out into the public away from the church?"

Emily stood silent for a split second. "James Winston may have a darker history of his abuse. But if it is an inside family secret. We may never find out why."

"There is one way to lure him out. Someone in the family has to make a positive identification of the body."

"The question is? Who will that be? John, I need a break. Want to go visit Robbie?"

"Why not. That little fella needs some love too."

Emily, John, and Buzz walked away from the scent of death.

Quiet silence overtook the ride to the hospital. The will of survival and thoughts about the past deaths inside of a cemetery never faded from the voice or thoughts of the time.

John Holmes was not satisfied with the interruption of his conversation with James Winston. Yet the head priest was either protecting the church or hiding the truth. Review the conversation and thoughts of James Winston. Reshaped the image of the priest during the conversation. Searching for a weakness in his character.

Emily on the hand. Began to re-examine the autopsy of Jackson Winston. Piece by piece. She reviewed her work. Trying to figure out any possible missing link in his death.

Buzz lay still in the back seat.

The conscience of between life and death searched for more answers.

John parked outside of the hospital. Buzz reared up his head. Tail began to wag. As if he sensed this was a place to be excited about. Obedient to Emily's commands. Sat and waited to be released. "Come on big boy."

A scene out of the Three Musketeers occurred. Three swashbucklers walked side by side into the hospital. The sense of joy became a smile on Emily's face. Her heart pounded thinking about Robbie. Just outside of the baby ward. Buzz became excited. There was one single scent inside of his nose. It was a reminder of a baby. Ran around the nurses until he found Robbie. Sat down waiting for Emily. Emily walked over and feed him a snack. Buzz sat down beside Robbie's bed. Emily leaned over and kissed him on the cheek. A nurse passed by with a bottle. Handed it to Emily. Picked him up. Began feeding Robbie. Humming a song from her childhood. Robbie smiled as he nursed on the bottle. She rocked him back and forth until. He fell asleep in her arms. John Holmes watched her motherly compassion. Admired Emily. Taking all the time in the world to be with one little angel. John secretly filed the paperwork to gain custody of Robbie. Figured it would be the surprise of her life. Robbie was the perfect balance in her life. After all the things that happen to her in the past.

Campbell spent the night observing the coming going outside of the church. Noticed a few old men, who passed in and out of his life. Wondered about the gathering and meeting. Maybe it was a church meeting. Sat admiring the stars and moon above. No one returned from the church right away. Finally, three hours later the same group exited from the church. No one from the staff of the church appeared. But one odd thing happened. A one figure finally walked out of the church. Campbell took a picture of the man. Someone he never saw or knew walked out of the church. Completely disappeared into the dark of night. Wished for a camera to expose the one person. Who may have overseen this cycle sex and death? Sadly, the one opportunity was lost. Trapped sitting alone in a cemetery. Then the unusual manifestations occurred. Jack Winston walked out. Creating a possible link between the children's death or a link to a pedophile group. Campbell decided to stay. Thinking it could possibly expose a link or possible answer as to why Jack Winston left the church. Sun light created over the dark horizon. The outside door was slightly exposed. Jack Winston reappeared. Walking back inside of the church. Campbell calculated. He was gone for over an hour. Enough time to meet with someone.

Considering he was not carrying any type of package with him. Campbell texted John Holmes. About Jack Winston movement early in the dawning hours. Ask John Holmes to meet him at the station. John Holmes asked Campbell to meet him at the morgue around eight. Decided not to share the information with anyone for the time being.

John Holmes explained the situation with Emily. She should drive herself to work for now. He would arrive later in about thirty minutes. Decided to make one more phone call. Ask for Officer Tom Flanagan to meet him at the morgue.

John Holmes stood outside. Patiently waiting for Flanagan. A police cruiser arrived. A tall lanky grey hair officer in his late fifties stepped out. Brushed off his uniform trying to look formal. John Holmes smiled. "I don't think that is necessary Tom. I have a job for you."

Campbell parked right beside Flanagan. Walked toward the other two men. "Good morning."

Flanagan spoke. "Bad morning Campbell?"

"No, I did an all nightery. Had to report to Detective Holmes."

"It seems. We something in common today."

John Holmes interrupted the cross examination of Campbell. "Tom, go inside and introduce yourself to Emily and wait. Campbell and I have to discuss a case."

Tom Flanagan understood the code of ethics and a reason to cover your butt. Without anyone around you. But it also meant an investigation was on going with limited access.

"Okay Campbell, tell me all of it." Campbell began explaining the night before. Concerning everything that happen. The most damaging statement was Jack Winston leaving and coming back later.

John Holmes stood silent. Considering the things being shared by Campbell. "We have to figure out his movement. This will require a lot more surveillance. I guess we will both take hand in this. One observing the church. The other one following Jack Winston. What do you think?"

"I am game for it. Pick one. It is your choice."

John Holmes breathed out and sighed. "You have lived her longer. I want you to follow him. I will do the other part. Do a good job, Campbell."

"Sounds good."

"Alright go home and sleep. Could be a long night or short one. May take more days too." John Holmes smiled. Walked inside of the morgue.

Campbell sighed. Smiled after the smile from John Holmes. Decided to call it a day.

John Holmes open the door. Peered out of a window. Insuring Campbell had left the parking lot.

Turned around and walked back into the morgue. Flanagan sat at a desk with Buzz under his feet. Of course, Buzz knew the footsteps. Jumped up and walked directly at John Holmes. Blocking hm from entering the morgue. John Holmes reached into his jacket. Offered Buzz a treat. This time Buzz refused to move. "So, Buzz. Your mama did not feed you huh?"

"Yes, Mama did. You forgot to feed him too. See Flanagan is treating him to the treat jar. Needless to say. That belly is dragging the floor. I suggest. You step around him or take him outside for a run." Emily smirked at John Holmes. As if he were the blame.

"Come on fat boy. Your mama has spoken. Come along Flanagan. You need to understand the moocher."

Flanagan followed John Holmes outside of the morgue. Patiently waited for an explanation.

"You are here to protect Emily. As you know. The cemetery outside of the church has provided the police department with a lot of bodies of children. From the past and present day. Emily is doing the autopsies right now. But a few usual events have surfaced. I want him to protect her and stay here for now. Buzz is her dog. He is important to her job and life."

Tom Flanagan spoke softly. "Detective Holmes, I will protect her with life. As you know. I have always done my job. Please I expect you to share the truth."

"Tom, I am afraid someone may try to stop her. A lot of dark secrets are being uncovered. Please do your utmost to protect her and Buzz. That dog is her life."

Tom Flanagan smiled. "You have my word. I will protect her and Buzz with my life."

John Holmes shook his hand. "I know you will. I selected this man for the job. Take care of them for me. I have work to do at the church. Please make sure she gets home safe too." John Holmes walked away. Never spoke another word. There was no reason to suspect Flanagan of failing him.

Emily observed the two men sharing their conversation. Understood Tom Flanagan was there for one reason to protect her and Buzz. Waited for Tom Flanagan to come back with Buzz.

"Well big boy, did you do your business and steal a snack? Officer Flanagan. Thank you for staying with me. I know John asked you too."

"Young lady. I am here to protect you and Buzz. Detective Holmes made sure of that. I am to escort you home too."

First call me Emily. Second, I know all the details. John only picks the best. I am in good hands. So, coffee and chair for you. There is a newspaper. Buzz will alert us of anyone snooping around."

"Emily, I would trust him with my life. I have seen him work. So, Buzz will be the guard and I will back him up."

Emily smiled. Kissed him on the cheek. "You are. Just like my father." Turned around. Went back to work.

Flanagan rubbed his cheek. Reminded him of his daughter. A forgotten memory. She pasted away at sixteen. But Emily treated her safety to loving father not a police officer.

Emily hid her emotions from death. The pain and emotions were buried under the sound of music. Humming and singing along to the sounds of life. The hand-written observations were detailed to the point. The autopsies proved to be painful. Her past captivity with Christopher Robin also interfered with her thoughts. But the detail reports were professional. Having John Holmes in her life proved to be the best medicine too. Buzz curled up in a corner on a blanket. Sound asleep and snoring. Sometimes he would sit under her worktable. Observing the mystical princess of his life. She would drop snacks for him daily. Go outside breaks and fresh air. Buzz chased the rabbits for fun. Officer Flanagan found her to be a refreshing break from police work. Emily sang and danced around with Buzz. Throwing a ball to him. Everything revolved around Buzz and her emotional life surrounded by death for the moment. A few days later the outside event changed.

Flanagan sensed someone was around. Steering clear of being detected. The odd occurrence stirred his emotional compassion to protect Emily and Buzz. One day it all changed. Noticed someone observing the tree of them. Hidden in a set of bushes. Turned around slightly motioned Emily inside. Emily treated as if it was time to go back to work. Buzz followed her. Flanagan was not far behind. Locked the door. Eased around a closed window blind. Pushed to the side. Trying to locate the unseen visitor. No one appeared. Called John Holmes to come by at the end of the shift. Instead of taking Emily home.

John Holmes parked beside the building. Walked inside. Pretending as if nothing was wrong. To avoid any type of distraction. In case the stalker was still around. "Flanagan, got anything on our stalker?"

"No. I took Emily home. Never came back. I decided to let you figure it out. How we are going to protect Emily. Figure out a way to catch the stalker. No need to draw attention to the person. Who has been outside?"

"Emily did anyone followed you. Notice anything different?"

"No one follows me to work. When I am outside. Buzz does his business by the same bush. Comes back over and sits with me."

Flanagan spoke quickly. "Buzz has a good nose. Buzz has had contact. That is a natural emotion. Instinct is to protect Emily from the unknown or someone. Who has been around her before?"

John Holmes thought about it for a long time. "Okay. Tomorrow same route. Emily let Buzz do his duty. Campbell and I will be at each end. Observe our stalker. Wait for him to leave or stay."

Emily listened to the conversation. "John, how do you know if this person will return?"

"My gut feeling alone. A stalker is never far away. But our stalker is here. For a different reason. So far. No malice intent at all. I think. This may be our messenger from the church."

Flanagan spoke. "John, if this is the messenger. Why is it happening now?"

"For some unknown reason, the church is hiding it. Does not want any type of exposure. I think. Someone is about to make contact. Not sure how."

Emily stared down at Buzz. "My good man. Tomorrow is your day. You are going to protect me too. Buddy's spirit seems to be guiding you too. So, make me proud too. Be Buddy tomorrow."

"I don't think you have to worry. Buzz just ignored you. Leaving all of us for a bush." Flanagan pointed at the same bush. Only this time Buzz sat down.

"Scent of death. Buzz does not act like that."

John Holmes waved everyone back. "Stand up with hands over your head."

James Winston stood up and walked out of the bushes.

"Buzz only does that if the victim is laying down. Emily. Like father like son. Buzz truly is a great detective." John Holmes motioned him to walk forward. James Winston stopped. "Place your hands at your side. Let us talk."

Emily slapped him on the face. "You had no right stalking me. You could have opened the door and came inside."

Flanagan and Holmes stood silent. Admiring her courage and anger at the same time.

"James, come inside. I want to ask you why? I do not want any lame brain excuses." Emily escorted James Winston inside.

Holmes and Flanagan smiled. Shrugging their shoulders.

"John, she has a lot character. But her tact is quite unforgiving. What do you think?"

"I think. She may be small. But I would took take her for granted. She packs quite a punch for a woman."

"Are you two coming?"

"Oh. Yes." Both men followed her inside. Staying close behind.

Emily shoved a stool over to Jack Winston. "Have a sit."

James Winston trembled and sat.

"Why have you been outside?"

"Because I wanted to talk with you. Hope you could help me. The church has forbidden me from speaking."

"What do you expect me to do? There are two police officers standing there. Maybe you should ask them."

"I need your help. To prove I am innocent. I did not kill my uncle."

"James, I know that. There is his body over there on the slab. I have been doing his autopsy."

"That is not enough. I need help. Please listen to me."

John Holmes whispered to Flanagan. "What is he afraid of?"

"Something is causing his fear. Someone has made a threat."

John Holmes nodded at Emily to continue. Emily thought about a way to convince Jack Winston to tell all. "Jack, tell me why you are here?"

"I need help."

"That is not an answer. I need a reason why? Are you afraid of someone? Is there more to this? Give answer. I will try to help you."

"The church wants me to not discuss this matter. I am afraid if someone finds out." James Winston concealed a lot of his thoughts.

"You know James. That is not an answer. I do not have time to baby sit you and your inconceivable weakness and fear of the church. So, you either tell me the truth or go home."

Tom Flanagan smiled. John Holmes enjoyed her power.

Emily patiently waited for an explanation. "Well."

James Winston stood still. Contemplated a reason why? "I have lied to you. The church is not involved. My father asked me not to talk about my uncle. There are too many reasons and secrets about my uncle. A lot of people want it pushed under the rug. They know. I know about the church meetings and the other things." James Winston spoke about the reasons. But did not offer any evidence.

"James, you want help from me. Tell the truth about the things that happen. Those things also surround your dead uncle. Whatever you are afraid of is going to kill a lot more children. Pick your poison family or children."

John Holmes admired her courage. Flanagan smiled. "What a fiery young woman. I think. She will win this argument."

"Damn right. She will win."

James Winston stood silent. Realized. The one thing in his life was also part of his past. One thing to consider was the truth or leave. Sat down on a stool beside of the cold stainless-steel slab. Staring at a young child's hand. Touched the hand of a child. Cried.

Emily witness a young man falling into the actual truth about life. There was no honor in lying. Hiding behind the family name. Already created the shame and disgrace of life from his uncle. Darkest decision of his life was staring him in the face. It was the truth.

John Holmes motioned Flanagan to follow him outside. Flanagan followed him. Neither man spoke a word. Until the door closed behind them.

"James, the space between us and the truth. Is now in Emily's hands. We no longer have a voice in it. I am afraid."

Tom Flanagan stood silent for a long period of time. "John, Emily is the only link. We must trust her instincts. She has a burden far greater than the truth. She must find his weakness. In order to find the truth. We are no longer a part of this investigation. Only Emily can forge the truth. Jack Winston needs a motherly woman. Emily has that instinct in her. Let her do it."

"Flanagan, you sound like her father. Then again. You are a father." John Holmes needed some fatherly advice about a woman.

"No John. You are in love that woman. It also shows between you two. I was not born yesterday. I have three grown kids and lost one. Emily is like a daughter. I have grown fond of her. She touched my heart. I needed that too. So have faith in her. She is going to change your life forever. Besides there are no secrets. Everyone knows about you two." Patted John on the shoulders and laughed him.

"Thanks. I thought no one knew. She is quite a young lady too." John smiled.

"John, you suffered to long with the loss of your wife. Emily saw it in you. But she also knew. What she wanted out of life. That little girl grew up. She sat there a long time with you. Before saying good-bye. I sat in the police car outside. Watched every moment of that long goodbye. She loved and trusted you. For caring about her that day. You also protected her. From the final moments of Alan Poe's death. Only you two know the dark secret between that man and child. No one will ever question you. But remember one day. You two will have to confront the truth. Solve the reasons and why. She was held captive."

"You know a lot. I was the one in charge. The day he died. The house is still locked up. You need to finish the investigation into the reasons. Why a child lived there."

"I guess you are right. Where are the files?"

"Locked up in that house. I never let anyone in there. I figured one day. You and I would go through it. But I think you and Emily need to finally close this case. I had a judge. I know seal the files for you. That is why, no one can go inside of the house. Besides, I have the keys." Flanagan reached into his pocket. Handed over the keys to John Holmes. "Your case now."

"No, it is our case. Emily wants answers too. She came back to find closure for a lot of families. Well?"

"Alright. This one is for Emily."

John Holmes found more than a friend. He found a man. Who found hope in Emily and a long-lost daughter? Who disappeared and died before her time?

Emily stood silent. Listen to the sound of breathing. It grew deeper. She never spoke a word. It was time for jack Winston to confess. If he wanted her help.

James Winston listen to the empty echo of his on breathing. The young woman in front of stood still. Never blinked an eye or shown any type of emotions. Realized she had no sympathy for his antics or fear. Sudden change in mood came. "All right. You are not talking. I am not going to tell you anything else."

Emily motioned him toward the door.

"Oh, you want me to go outside and face the police." Stubbed his foot.

"I personally don't care. Which one you pick. Those two-gentleman standing outside. Will be a lot harder to deal with. Pick your poison. I really do not care. One way or the other." Emily sat down at her desk. Ignored him. Buzz laid down at her feet.

James Winston was trapped. It was of his own making. There was no exist. "What do you want?"

Emily smiled. Jack never saw or noticed. Her confidence. She was here for a win and wanted his failure. "Time to talk. I have no desire to listen to your self-pity."

James Winston almost stomped his feet. Instead. He found a stool. Sat down. "Okay. Now what?"

"What do you mean by now what? I told you. It was time to talk. What more do I need to explain? I want the truth from you."

"All my life. I have told to tell the truth. I am now trying to do it. You ask me to tell the truth. Maybe I should leave." Stood up and walked toward the door.

"Here let me help you leave." Emily open the door. "John and Flanagan. Your suspect is ready to leave."

James Winston was stunned. Never expecting the two men to be waiting for him. Turned around. "Now what do I do?"

"A simple choice me or those two."

James Winston silence incurred the truth. No longer able to run away from the two men outside and the truth. Suddenly broke down like a crying baby. "Forgive me, god. For I have sinned before your eyes. Have mercy om soul."

Emily suddenly slapped his face. "I dare you. Invoking god's name to protect yourself from failure. Do you see the dead children? In this morgue. I have seen every one of them. My heart cries for them. Not one of them lived beyond their ages to become adults. You demented little bastard. Are you the one? Who shares children with perverted old men? Leave them to die." Her reactions were the reminders of her captive life. Six months of a living hell. Contemplating murder to be free. But the pages of life also provided a better solution. A dying man's compassion to help fulfill her life.

James Winston stunned by her attacks on his life. "Why are you so cruel? I did not offer one single child. I was one of them!"

John Holmes and Tom Flanagan heard his confession. Both men stood outside of the crack door. Both men knew it was time to save Emily from her pain and compassion. Door opened. Jack Flanagan took Emily away. Holding her close as she cried. John Holmes took charge of the Jack Winston.

"You caused enough heartache and pain. Your selfish behavior is just as unforgiving as the truth. You decided to share with Emily. Just now. Do you want to continue or walk away?" John Holmes knew and understood his weakness. Jack Winston brutal confession would also lead to a confession about his actual childhood. The dark side would expose the truth of his life.

"I am waiting for an answer."

James Winston realized. There was no way out. John Holmes held him accountable. Just for the way. He used Emily. Knew Flanagan would not allow him to leave too. Being held captive for lying was now a major problem. "What happens if I refuse?"

"I will charge you with a crime. Deception and lying to an officer of the law. If you walk out. I will charge you as a fugitive too."

Flanagan decide to block the exit.

John Holmes smiled. The false narrative of keeping him. Also unsettled his thoughts. Felt the pressure of being unable to run. Heard another voice.

Emily spoke. "Let him go. He hides behind his family and the church. The decision is now his to make. I think the little coward will run far. He lacks the character of being a responsible priest. When the truth comes out. The church will not protect. Their good name would suffer from his weakness. A priest is a pillar of strength. Not a cowardly little man." Emily preyed upon his character and weakness as a human being. If he was dedicated to the priesthood. A truth follower of Christ. He would not sin before God's eyes.

Flanagan opened the door. Allowing the sun light to enter. It was a shallow attempt to insure. God would offer him redemption. One last time.

John Holmes felt the compassion of the devil. Jack Winston was not going to dictate the terms of his life or death. "James, you spent time with Emily. She tried to help you. Now you want to run away. "Why?"

"I do not owe you a thing. I came here of my own free will. You think. I will bow down to you. This is extortion. I know my rights.!"

"Damn. Right. You got a choice. Run. See how far you will get. Someone out there is watching you. Someone from the church or family is going to stop you. I do not care. Go." John Holmes played on hie emotions.

"I don't believe you. I am safe from all things. I trust my faith."

"Save your baptism of life for the afterlife. Now leave the morgue. I do not want to waste my time any longer." John Holmes turned around and winked at Emily.

"You really don't care. If I live or die."

"Jack, I am not pointing a gun at your head. You can imagine anything. I have work to do. Flanagan, show him out."

Flanagan pushed the door open. Motion him toward the sunlight. "Have a nice day." Flanagan noticed something unusual.

James Winston walked away. Toward the open door. Flanagan shut it.

"What are you doing?"

"Saving your life. You want to go out or stay?" Flanagan winked at John Holmes. John turned around to face Emily. Placed a finger on his lips. The decoy worked to perfection. Emily smiled.

The tethering disguise of life and death hung high over Jack Winston's thoughts. Fear created an imaginary darkness of death. The conviction of death created a moment. Disguised as the devil casting one last ditch effort of instilling fear in the soul of a boy priest. "Can you protect me?"

"Sure. No problem. Tell me about the children in the cemetery."

"The only answer lies on a slab of steel over there. I can only share the things I know."

"I suggest you start talking. Anything but the truth. Will get you in trouble with law. Do we understand each other?" John Holmes did not mince his words.

James Winston had no way out of this situation. Nor did he a way to lie. "I understand. May God have mercy on me."

Emily interrupted him. "God will share his mercy. The day you tell the truth and ask forgiveness. So, stop hiding behind the vale. Of lies." Sadly, she saw the fears of a young man. Engulfed with his on secret regrets. The pain would come one step at a time.

John Holmes showed little emotions. Never regretted being a tough cop. Put aside his emotions to find the truth and justice.

Beyond the pale rider of death and justice rode the same horse. No would ever hear the silence of justice calling out the forgotten children. Who died by the hands of pedophiles?

Flanagan walked over to Jack Winston. Placed his hand on his shoulder. Spoke, like a father to him. "Jack, today you must face the truth. You are no longer a child or priest. You are the only voice of hope and justice. Time to become a full-grown man. No one will defend you and treat you like a child anymore. Please understand.

You are the only one to defend those children. Lying before you in this morgue."

James Winston knees buckled. Flanagan held him up. Tears rolled over the edges of his eyes. Sorrow was not his weakness. Hope was not his salvation. Jack Winston stood before the one thing. He had never faced. Being a child. Who suffered from being raped by his uncle? "I was raped by my uncle. For years he fondled me. Took me on vacations to abuse me. One day my father caught him. Hired a bunch of men to castrate him. During this time period. The F.B.I. used him to convict pedophiles. It was his revenge. But the act of being a man. Without a conscience. Profited off the F.B.I. too. Moved here for protection. No one ever checked up on him. The face of revenge exposed the wealth and acts of child molesters in the state for profit. The activities at the church were meetings. The closed doors of were used to exploit the church. So, no one would find out. Donations were made to the church for the use of the meeting room. I do not know. Who murdered him?"

Emily slapped him. John Holmes grabbed her. "Stop! Your anger will not save the past. Your work will save children from the future." Emily collapsed into his arms and cried. John Holmes walked her outside. Silence filled the morgue.

Flanagan stood still. Before he decided to speak. "You are a victim James. But the real victims are all around this room. Emily is a victim too. She is the one person. Who sees this day in and out? You broke her heart and soul today. I am personally. Going to insure, your safety and protect you. But I will not allow you to run from the truth. Do we understand each other?"

James Winston felt cold chills. The grim reaper of life and death had confronted him. Tom Flanagan's grim reminder was the one thing. Jack Winston would fear.

John Holmes held the lost child one more time. She cried in his arms. No longer feeling the joy of life. The compassion dripped with tears of sorrow. "Stand here. Do not move." Released her. Walked back inside. "Flanagan. Take him to the church. Do not allow him to leave. I will be back later."

"No problem. You heard the man. Move out." Two different men walked side by side. One with bold courage and the other living in fear.

John Holmes walked away. Never turning back to listen to the conversation. Took Emily by the arm and called Buzz. Together the three of them drove away. Emily sat silent and in pain and sorrow. Buzz sat staring over the seat at his beloved master. John Holmes quietly drove away. Turning away from home. Drove directly to the hospital. Open the door and allowed the Emily and Buzz out. "Listen to me. There is a child inside. He needs you to love on him. Now go inside. Buzz and I will wait outside in the fresh air."

Emily wiped away the tears and smiled. John Holmes pushed her toward the door. Thought about Paul Simons song. Mother and Child reunion. Buzz wandered around the parking lot. Minding his own business and doing his business.

Emily sat down with Robbie. Cuddling him and singing a song to comfort herself and Robbie. Feeding him a bottle of milk. A slight twinkle of love and smile. Reflected off the pure innocence of a angel. Who comforted a lost child from the past? Sometimes the child of the past and present are the same person. Life is a gift to be shared between mother and child. Emily found compassion in being that child. Saw a reflection of life before her. The day her parents came to comfort and take her home. Another reflection of life touched her soul. A tall dark hair police officer. Sending her on her way home. Today the same man sent her on her way home to a bundle of love. Little did she know, A dog and a man witness her love and compassion near the door. Sound of silence proved to be the cure of a broken heart. Robbie slept quietly in her arms. She rocked him back and forth. Time heals all wounds. But the passion of love cures all pain. Emily found peace within a tiny heart and a grown man.

Emily stood up. Placed Robbie in his bed. Kissed his forehead. Turned around. Seeing two complete big babies smiling at her. "Come on you two big babies. Thank you, John."

John Holmes just smiled. "Going to take you home for the day. You two are off duty. I am going to the church."

John Holmes drove away from home. Leaving Emily with her faithful companion. Stopped outside of the church entrance. Stared at the cemetery. Uncomfortable emotions returned. Final inspection of the grounds seemed empty. What was missing from the investigation?

Campbell walked toward him.

"How long have you been here?"

"When I can't sleep. I come here. Trying to figure out the reason for being here. Nothing makes any sense. All the bodies over the past years. The fresh bodies found out here. Why such a long timetable? No one seemed to care or investigate it. Who or what is behind it? Nothing adds up. Why?"

John Holmes realized. Why? Sitting there. This is not about the church. It is about some one's past life. A single person's identity. Part of this revelation are the bodies. The other part is a secret identity. "Campbell, do you know any of the people?"

"No. Not one single one of them. The meetings have been held twice. Same people move in and out. None of them leave together or enter together."

"When was the last time? You saw them." John Holmes felt let down. But the surprise of a group coming and going. It was a bit unusual.

"Three days ago. Come around nine at night and leave in about twenty minutes. No one in the church is around here or near them." Campbell almost felt like it was a letdown.

John Holmes thought about it. "This is not about pedophiles. This is about covering up something or someone. I have a feeling. There is a pedophile ring of people. Molesting and accidental killings or a pleasure kill. But the group of unknowns is something else. We may have two different reasons for all of this. Someone maybe involved in the cover up of the pedophiles. But the other is to cover up one man's murder."

"That one man is Jackson Winston. Who died out here? Who did it?" John Holmes hoped it would end there.

The past few nights were long and tedious hours of failure. No one came or went. Both men wondered if the opportunity came and went. Was it too late? Edge of darkness creeped over the entrance covered in fog. "If Jack the Ripper was alive? This would be the perfect moment."

"A morbid thought huh Campbell."

"No. I read a lot of books. I studied crimes from the past. Jack the Ripper was quite interesting."

"Do you have any more of those dark secrets to tell?"

"None that I know of."

"Criminal denial too." John Holmes smiled. The sarcasm was also an insult too.

"Do you think the group of unknown men are covering up for someone?"

John Holmes pondered the thought. "Campbell, you may have solved the reason for the committee of men coming and going."

"Why?"

'That is one reason. We are going to stay here. To confront the men. Who are meeting here?"

The hours of time ticked slowly away. The long-awaited moment came true. One by one the men filled into the church. Finally, no one else came or went. John Holmes open the door. "Time for a confession."

Side by side two men walked into the shadows of darkness. Onward into the shadows of the unknown. Would one single man decide to confess the reasons for the ongoing meetings. Pushed the door open. Walked down toward a dimly lit room. Pushed the door open. All the men turned around to face their accusers.

"I am Detective John Holmes. This is officer Campbell. I have a few questions for all of you."

Grey haired man stood. "Please go ahead. We have nothing to hide."

"As you may know. There is an ongoing investigation outside in the cemetery. I was wondering if anyone of you. Might have an answer?"

"What may that be. I am sure. We have nothing to hide from you detective."

"Someone has been burying young boys out there for a quite a few years. But lately someone has decided to add more. I was wondering about it. You gentleman come here late at night. Under the secrecy of the darkness it seems."

"All the men laughed. This is a night of relief. Our wives tend to nag us too much. As you may well know. Man needs time to himself. Plus, we discuss sports and play poker."

John Holmes laughed. "I guess. When I am older. I will try to do the same. But one more question please."

"Please continue. We will be glad to assist you." The old men laughed.

"I guess. It is sort of funny too. But have you ever noticed? Anyone strange outside at night. When you are here?"

"On few occasions. An old man would walk among the graves. Mumbling prayers out there. Figured he was lost intime over a loss. Sorry."

"Thank all of you gentleman for the time. I hope the game is winner take all."

A round of laughter struck the air.

John Holmes smiled. Campbell followed him outside.

"I think maybe that one man was Jackson Winston."

"But who would want Jackson Winston dead?"

"Revenge is one thing. The other is. Why would an old man without any sexual way to assume? His past lifestyle of molesting children. Be the victim of murder. Because someone's past is woven into this whole case."

"James Winston is one. My father's past is two. Big mama is three. Mary Jane Hudson father is number four."

John Holmes smirked at the reasons. But also held back at the same time. "Your father is dead. The file gives us only a few answers. Mama protected someone. Mary Jane Hudson father is a man. With a very dark past and is protected by a file with no answers. The other part is still an unanswered question surrounding the church. Why is Jack Winston being protected by the church?"

"Because our choir boy knows a lot about this mystery. I have known him sense high school."

John Holmes almost exploded. But held back his anger. "Campbell tell me your family's dark past. Leave nothing out this time."

"From the first day I found that file. It was a constant threat into my past life and my dad's secret life. My father protected a lot people in the city government. Witness a lot of things in the church. Witness the coming and going of little boys and girls. Being an up standing man of god and the church. Required his silence. The silence was bought and paid for by the church."

"Who over saw the church at the time? One singular member with total power. It was not the priest. It was the mayor. But the mayor was not a pedophile. Money played a big part in this charade of life inside of the church."

"Whose money was it? Why did it happen?" John Holmes began to hear a story. The nonconsensual affairs of having sex with children. Turned his stomach.

"I do not know the complete story. I only witness it one or two times. My father took me with him a few times."

John Holmes sensed. There was more to the story. Campbell hid more of the past. For some reason. It was a situation. That somewhere in time would need an answer. "For the time being say nothing." John Holmes decided to end the evening. See me tomorrow at the morgue."

Campbell walked away without a word. Sensing the entire incident was not over. Tried to figure out a way to close it.

John Holmes heard enough for now. But Campbell was going to explain the entire incident one way or the other. Stood still under the shadow of darkness. Studying the window above. Only a dark shadow of space covered the window. Someone stepped out of the shadows of darkness.

"Good evening Detective Holmes. Care to walk with me."

"Why not. I have nothing to lose. One way or the other."

"I watched you from afar in the window. Your work habits fit your image. But our conversation isn't complete yet."

"So, you pick this hour in time. To Confront me."

"No. I am not confronting you. Time to share a few thoughts and blessings. I hope you do not mine?"

"Well somethings are better said. Then not at all."

"You are quite the scholar of wisdom. I hope it comes with an answer."

"Let start with the gentlemen in the church. I set you up. I figured. It was time to have a conversation alone with you. Campbell served my purpose well. I simply wanted a reason for all this until you found the souls of children."

"So. A man of conscience decides to appear before me. Go ahead."

The priest smiled. "The past is a difficult thing to accept. Present day stories and a live child is quite a scare. But the child is good hands now. I hope you raise him well."

"You have my word. Tell me more about the past and present."

"The sins of the past are the churches sins. But I searched the archives of the church records. There are sinners in the boundaries of God's past on these holy grounds. Most are buried within the grounds. But a few sinners of the past. Still exist in the pages of time. I insured that the files would turn up for you to investigate. Campbell's father confessed his sins to me. I was a young priest. Gave me the files. Told me. He placed a few unaccounted pieces of evidence. I did not know. His son would be the one to find them. I am to blame for his pain and suffering. Please forgive the child of the father. I am about to give you a complete file and record of the past. You will find the names and records of the victims. Also, the perpetrators of the crimes committed against the children. It has been a long difficult time for me. But I am free of this weight on my shoulders."

John Holmes stood silent. "I never thought about it. Until now. You may have been high above me. But the truth fell to earth. I want to thank you for caring about all those children. I hope your life is filled with blessings too."

"I am sure you will find all the answers. To a few more lost souls too." The priest turned away. Walked back into the shadows of the church.

John Holmes gripped the file. The long-lost past had found the present. A somber quiet evening found the solemn words of hope and peace.

Emily quietly prepared dinner. Humming a baby song. Her mother always sang to her. John Holmes listen to the sweet sensual compassion of a heart felt moment between a mother and child.

"I see. Your heart waning and wanting a certain little man. Did you ask Buzz if it was okay?"

"Buzz is a good sitter. I am sure Robbie will drive him crazy. How was your night?"

John laid the file on the table. "Everything you and I want to know. Is inside of this file. The priest handed this old file. It seems Campbell's father gave him the file. Before he passed away. He planted a file inside of the desk. Campbell found it. The rest is history."

Emily took the file. Sat down and began to read it. "Do you know? What is inside of here?"

"I gave it to you. The history inside is part of the investigation and identity of all the victims."

"John, how am I going to fix all the damage? All of these children have no family or friends to give them their final rest."

"Emily, just your work and dreams will cover the pages of history. Your compassion and love will be a monument to the truth. I will back you. Stand by you. Not one single child will be forgotten. I promise. But first you must build a case for me. I need all the help and answers to do this."

Emily walked over and held on to John Holmes. "We will finish this. I promise."

John Holmes sat down. Felt the world grumbling around his thoughts. Emily sat down beside him. Held his hand. "You are not alone. I am here." Pulled him into her heart and soul. The fragile balance of life. Was being held together by two souls.

Sun rose upon the dark dreams of the night before. John Holmes found Emily and Buzz sleeping on top of him on the couch. "Come on sleepy heads get up. I can't breathe."

Emily rolled Buzz onto the floor. Sat up staring into his face. "You need a shave and bath. Get up."

"Thanks. I love you too." John walked to the shower. Stood under the hot water and shaved. Washed away the scent off from the night before. Dressed and walked out to breakfast. Picked up Emily and delivered her to the shower. "Okay stinky. It is your turn." Left her standing in the shower.

"Come Buzz breakfast."

A scent of a woman appeared. Dressed in jeans and a pink flowered shirt. "Good morning boys."

John poured her coffee. Kissed her cheek. "I am going to take you to the morgue. Campbell is meeting me there."

Emily smiled and kissed him. "You are the best thing to happen to me. It was worth waiting for you. Even if you were a hard nose cop. The day you gave me that phone. Buddy seemed to love you. He never cared you sat down by me. Never sat between us. He knew a lot about your love too." She stood on her tip toes and kissed him. "Come on boys. Time to go to work."

"Good morning Flanagan. How are you?" Emily kissed his cheek.

Flanagan smiled and hugged her. "I am fine."

"Go ahead and assist Emily. I am waiting for Campbell. Emily will fill you in today. I hope you can share some insight in the file. She has."

"No problem John. Anything else?"

"No. I trust your wisdom and your knowledge of this file." John Holmes hoped. Flanagan could share some insight to the file.

Campbell drove up and parked. John Holmes motioned for him to come inside. "Good morning. I have information. Last night I had a visitor from above. The priest gave me. Your father's real file. He planted the other file under the desk. Your father gave it to him before he died. It contains a full list of the victims. A few names of the individuals involved. Emily will research the file. Identify the victims from the information. I hope. We can provide a proper burial for all of the children."

Campbell stood in shock.

"I am sorry. But this is the truth. I have all the respect for you and your father. But Campbell, the time has come to find the facts and faces of this crime. I am going to use the full aspect of the law to arrest and punish every one of them." John Holmes stood silent.

Campbell finally spoke. "I am sorry. I never realized that my father knew. Hid so much information. I hope we can finish this." Campbell broke down and cried. John Holmes guided him to a chair. Emily gave him a cloth. To wipe away the tears. Nothing could possibly take away the pain.

Flanagan whispered into his ear. "Your father was a good man. He free of the secret. Finally, he will be honored. For being a good police officer. I will make sure of it."

Campbell pulled his self together. "What next John?"

"How much do you know about Jack Winston?"

"About ten years behind me in school. Everyone knew. Who his family was? The girls always hung around him. Something rather odd about him too. No one saw him around town. Some days he hung around with his creepy uncle. Almost as if he were tied to him. I know. His uncle was gay. But Jack never seemed to be happy around him. Maybe Jack was molested by his uncle."

John Holmes thought long and hard on that question. "What if his uncle molested him? Maybe his father found out. Emily check the identities of the pedophiles."

Emily open and read the list of people considered to be pedophiles. Nothing usual about the list. Flipped over the pages. Found a handwritten note. "Hold on for a minute. In case you have found my file. There is another file hidden in an old abandon church. Martha Jane will show you the church and the file."

"Who is Martha Jane?"

Campbell laughed. "Been a long time. Sense I heard that name."

Emily stomped her foot. "Campbell, one more time. Before I cut you open. Who is Martha Jane?"

Flanagan laughed. "Emily, my dear child. You know this woman. John knows this woman. Campbell can tell you too. You know her as Big Mama."

Emily stood silent. "The old man is her father. That is his church. Inside of that church is a file."

"I wonder why? Does Mama know more that she says?' John Holmes now had a decision to make.

Flanagan offered an answer. "John now is not the time to do anything. Emily must finish her work. The proof is in the pudding. As my mother once said."

John Holmes stood silent. "Okay. Flanagan is right. The fewer people, who know is the best option. Leave James Winston alone. I want to keep a lid on this situation."

Campbell decided to ask a question. "Are you going back to the old church?"

"No. I do not want to disturb the old man. Keep mama as far away as possible. No one is going near the Chain Gang or the bottoms."

The sound of silence engulfed the morgue. The last words of a defining moment became sealed. No one would speak or share the information the file. Until Emily sorted out all the information. Making a case for the arrests and judgment to come forth from a court of law.

"Flanagan, you take care of Emily and Buzz. Come on Campbell. Time to pretend we are investigating the cemetery. I want to observe the movements of James Winston."

Emily stood silent. Began reading the file. The investigation was a long-held secret. Campbell's father wrote down as much information as possible. Linking the affairs with dates and time. Emily found Mary Jane Hudson name in the file. Began to read the dates of arrival and departures from the pedophile list. A set of number figures with dollar signs around them. Notification of payment to her father. "Flanagan tell me about Mary Jane Hudson father. He listed in the file.

"Emily, I am sure you will ask more questions as it goes moves forward. Most of the rumors around town were about her being a prostitute. No one knew for sure if her father was selling her. She was fourteen at the time. A lot of stories were spread around school before she disappeared."

"Do you think she died?"

"No one knows for sure. I wish. I could answer that question. She was a wonderful child. Took great care to protect her sister. Funny thing about a year later. Her sister disappeared too."

"Do you believe she is alive?"

"I cannot say yes or no. But if you were her. Would you find a way to save your sister?"

"If I were her. I would have saved my sister. But then again. You tend to sidestep the truth too."

"Emily, there some mysteries in life. That are better left alone." Emily hugged Flanagan. Did not say another word about Mary Jane Hudson.

"Flanagan, did you ever hear about these stories in this file?"

"I heard a lot of stories as I grew up. No one at the police station ever spoke about it. I would say Campbell's father knew more about the dark secrets. Then anyone in this town. Why? I do not know."

"Do you think? He witnesses some of it." Emily tried hard to pry open Flanagan's thoughts.

"Little lady, right now. I am protecting your life. If that file goes public. A lot of people will search for the person. Who found it? John and you would be on their list to get rid of."

"I spent six months being captive to a serial killer. He shared his life and thoughts with me. I lived. Christopher Robin taught me. How to be a human being. I learned. How to survive a serial killer and a compassionate man. Who found a way to forgive me? Protect me from the evils of his thoughts and life. Provided me an education. Tell me. What not to fear. In his death. He found peace. But left behind a scar and victims. Now I am going to finish this file. Then I am going to try and find the victim's parents. In order to give them closure."

Flanagan smiled. "You are a tuff little girl. Perhaps you will find my daughter too."

Emily took his hand. "Come on dad. We have work to do."

Flanagan wiped away the tears from his eyes. Emily kissed his cheek. "I promise I will."

John Holmes walked around the cemetery. Searching for a few clues. Pushed and moved the soil around the graves. Campbell began to search around the bushes. Where the body was found? John stood silent. Observed the work of Campbell. Figured just maybe. There might be a clue around the area. Where the body was found? John

Holmes walked down the hill side. Studied each grave. The symbolic cross was another mystery. Perhaps someone was dropping off the victims to be buried. Suddenly he realized. The soil where Jackson Winston died was the same soil in the cemetery. "Campbell call forensics out here now."

Campbell turned around stunned. Made the call.

John Holmes called Emily. "Come to the cemetery. I need you to cross reference the soil with Jackson Winston and the fresh graves."

Emily stopped. "Come on Flanagan. Buzz. Wake up. We need to go the cemetery." Emily grabbed her bag of tools.

Flanagan followed her every move.

"Campbell search around the bushes. For any type of a fresh dig or if the bushes have been disturbed."

Forensics arrived. Emily was close behind. "Everyone gathers around me. I want every bush disturbed. Remove soil samples. Search for more bodies. Emily retake the samples on the hill from fresh graves. Cross reference the soil with the soil down below. Possibly more bodies too."

Emily called Buzz. Time to investigate the bushes. Buzz. Do your thing. Fine all the bodies please."

John. Turned around to look at the window. A familiar figure observed him. Only thing time. He signed the cross and saluted him. John Holmes clasped his hands together. Bowed to him. Symbolic gesture was a peaceful thought of forgiveness.

Emily followed Buzz. Buzz began to sniff and scratch at the soil. Until he sat down. Emily staked the bush. Call for a dig. Buzz sniffed around the bushes one by one. Emily staked a cross in front of the bushes.

John Holmes realized. Jackson Winston died. Somewhere else. The bodies were buried under the bushes. Someone else would bury them. Except the day Buzz found Jackson Winston. Everything moved in a different direction. Walked over to Emily and whispered. "The bushes are the drop point. Then someone else buries them."

"John, the problem is. The bodies being buried are recent. What if someone knew. Created this moment to engage the police. Tip the police off. About a crime being committed."

"Who could possibly know?"

Emily smiled. "Someone. Who already knew that answer? Had cover up their identity to prove it."

"Someone saved Robbie's life too. A shallow grave and air for him. The entire observation from heaven above. May have played a part in this too."

"Remember someone wanting revenge could have done it."

"There are two possible answers and maybe a third one too." John Holmes considered his suspects.

"Are going to share your thoughts with me?" Emily listened for an answer.

John Holmes smiled. "No. Not yet. To many ears around here. But I have a few thoughts to share with you later. The one person high above is not one of them. It is an outsider."

Emily began to analyze his thoughts. "Flanagan, shall we leave here now?"

"You are the boss. Make the call."

"John. We are going back to the morgue. Pick me up there."

Flanagan observed the conversation. "You two were quite animated. Something is a mist here. I think. John has finally found the clue to this mess."

"Flanagan, you have a third sense. Just like my father. You can read my face and expressions. I am sure you are quite will informed. After all you had kids."

"No. I am married too. I can read between the lines. When two people love each other. You two are quite the match for each other. Strong wills and compassionate emotions. But the balance is natural between you two. There is that twinkle in your eyes too. Seeing your future at thirteen. Must have been a shock."

"He was a tough hard nose cop. But the compassion he shared was unique. Never once did he stop watching me. As if he knew I was different. But in my youthful days of growing up. His memories would come and go back too that day. I thought about him too. I wondered if I would ever see him again. Then I found a chance and way to be around him. Here I am."

"Sometimes fate is the truth. You searched for the truth inside of your soul. Found that mystical soul. You came back to get it back."

"I sure did dad. I love your thoughts too. I hope you find time to be around Robbie too. He needs an old soul too."

"Are you asking me for something?"

"Yes. He needs a godfather and a grandfather too. Are you up to it?"

"Is this a permanent offer for life? If it is. I accept."

"Yes. It is."

Emily and Flanagan walked away. Headed back to the morgue.

John Holmes walked over to a concrete bench. Sat down alone. Searched the grounds for a reason and thought. Emily made more sense than he did. Who was the go between? Who set it all up? John Holmes knew the reason why. But the unexplained reasons as for why. Left an empty trail of thoughts.

A man dressed in black sat down beside of him. "Sometimes mysteries are reasons behind the truth."

"You know. This is our third civil conversation. So far. I am zero for two. Somehow I think you witness a lot of things. But you never were one of the lost souls. Am I missing something here?"

"May I call you John?"

"Why not? At least it is a good start."

"John, a vision of hope comes with the darkness. You sit here alone. God has prepared you for this quest. You found peace within your heart. She is a woman of great passion and love. I saw her break down. I saw her love a child. You should always give her love and hope. But remember this. Everything I have given you is the truth. You will solve it one piece at a time. The final piece will come with love and compassion. You will find a path into life. Dwell not on the past. But seek answers coming into focus. The moment of truth is now. The evil in men's heart will fall into the depths of hell for their sins. You are truly a blessed man. Forgive the loss in your heart. She shared her love of life with you. Gave you a far greater dream of life to fulfill."

John Holmes smiled. "I am sorry for treating the way I did. But you are right. I have a lot of anger. But it is not about you. It is the loss of love. Finding love from a child. I saved. She grew up into a woman. I will finish this. You will be saved from my failure of life. I truly thank you for your time. I hope in the future you will be able to bless our child.”

“You have already blessed the child. He has hope and love. You two will bless him with love. Now I must go about being a priest. Come one day and sit with me once again.” The priest signed the cross. Turned away to go inside.

John Holmes sat alone.

Campbell walked over and sat down. “Today has been a day of strange things and a few blessings.”

“Campbell, sometimes strange things are the reasons. For us to find answers. Tell me something you learned today.”

“John. For some strange reason. The graves were marked on purpose. The soil samples were clues. Someone was trying to tell us something.”

“Yelp. But first Emily must finish the soil samples. Then search for answers on the new graves. Buzz was a smarter detective than we were. Time to go home. See you back here in the morning.”

The final moment of the day was picking up Buzz and Emily. Open the door and walked into the morgue. Buzz nudged him. John gave him a treat. “Good evening.”

Flanagan laughed. “This young lady has been waiting for her escort. Do you have an excuse, Mister Holmes?”

“No sir. But my heart begs for forgiveness.”

Emily waltzed over and hung onto his neck. ‘Where is my reward?”

"I feed Buzz. What is next?" John Holmes kissed her. Turned back to Flanagan. "Why are you still here?"

"On my way. See you tomorrow Emily."

"Bye."

"Well. I think. We will go home. Call out for dinner. Sit down together."

"I am not sure about the sit down. Dinner would be nice. I think a hot bath would soothe my aches and pain too. If you are nice and sweet. I might share the bed with you."

"The power of persuasion is difficult to handle. You seem to have the upper hand here." John Holmes picked her up. Carry Emily to the door. Buzz barked at him. The moon over head seem to smile down the two lovers. The solid sound of thunder proved to be a distraction. Emily escorted Buzz out on to the couch. She smiled and kiss John. They wrapped around the night. Fell into deep sleep.

Early morning hours dripped with the sound of a moist morning rain. Sun light creeped over the window.

Emily stood under a hot shower alone. The scent of her fragrance bloomed under the sun light. John Holmes concentrated on the day before. Emily walked by draped in a towel. Dropped it to dress. Exposing the natural beauty of being a woman. John concentrated on her nude body. How elegant she had grown up from the days. He last saw her leaving her captive life behind. Never dreamed he would ever see her again. She turned around and smiled. "Good morning? You need to shower and clean up. We have a lot of work and thoughts to think about. Who is that one person?"

"Trying to figure why? Someone would do this. Lead us to the crime scene."

"First I need to solve the death of Jackson Winston. "Second you need to get dressed. I will make breakfast. While you shower and look like a police officer, Mister Holmes." Snapped a finger for Buzz to wake up. "Come sleepy head time for breakfast." Buzz climbed down off the chair. Followed her into the kitchen. Sat down by the stove. She cooked eggs and bacon. John Holmes smelled the scent of eggs frying. Poured two cups of coffee. Pitched a piece of toast to Buzz. Emily sat two plates on the table and one on the floor. Tilted John's head back and kissed him.

After breakfast John called Flanagan. To meet them at the morgue. Left Emily with Flanagan.

John Holmes strolled into his office. Searched for Campbell. "Campbell, time to work over at the church." John Holmes walked away toward the door. Campbell jumped from the chair. Headed out the door.

John smiled. "See the dogs panic. Everyone wants to know about last night."

"I felt the discomfort in the room. No one spoke to me."

"Alright, tell me your thoughts on James Winston and his uncle."

Campbell stood silent. "John, I think there is a deeper problem. How far did their relationship go? I figured the man might have been molesting him for years."

"Do you think James Winston killed his uncle?"

"Maybe. There is more here than meets the eyes. Who controlled the molestation of the children? We know it goes a long way back. But who is doing it now?"

"One thing is for sure. Someone is burying the children for a reason. Leaving clues for us to find. We never noticed the clue until we found Jackson Wilson."

"There is a third party. Trying to help us or finish off the ring of pedophiles." Campbell defined the two basic reasons.

"What if Mary Jane Hudson is still alive. She trying to help us."

"It would be a miracle to begin with. But there are no clues or answers. How would we ever know?"

"Someone is doing us a favor. They have shown us a lot of answers to be found. Whoever it is?" John Holmes measured the time frame of the murders from now to the past. If Mary Jane Hudson was alive. She would have an inside track. Capable of exposing a lot of people. John decided to call Emily.

"Hello."

"Are, there any type of fingerprints available? Could they possibly be matched to anyone?"

"John that is a long shot. Time to go to the church. Find out from the old man. Or you can try to back Mama into a corner at the church."

"How do you feel about all of this?"

"Time to force her hand. She hides a lot of things from the people around her and us. The old man could possibly fold and offer us the file." Emily decided to play a long shot. Hope one of the two would fold under the pressure.

"It is worth the afford and hope for the best. Bring your two bodyguards to the cemetery. Campbell and I will be waiting for you."

Emily smirked. "At least he warned her. So, she would not be surprised. "Be there as soon as possible. Good-bye." Emily realized John Holmes had a lot more on his mind. Wondered what he was searching for. "Come on Buzz and you to Officer Flanagan. John wants us at the cemetery right away."

"Shall we leave now, Emily?"

Emily smiled at Flanagan. "I love it. When a true gentleman asks your permission. Shall we exit sir?"

Flanagan laughed. "Thank you for the comic relief. It beats the boredom."

"Well, you are back on the street. What do you think of Buzz?"

"That is one beautiful dog. He is so polite and gentle."

"Do not let him fool you watch." Emily pulled out a snack. Buzz sat down and waited for it. "See what I mean. He will not move until. He eats the snack. Waits to see if there is more." Buzz just sat there. Emily flipped him one more. "Come Buzz time to work." Buzz followed her after she told him time for work.

"Buzz is still a beautiful dog, Emily. I am glad. I got to know both of you."

"Buzz is a cadaver dog. He has an uncanny sense of locating dead people. Was trained to be one. I was in college. Buzz reacted different to death. My professor told me to take him to school. I have a best friend and great cadaver dog too. We are going to the cemetery. Come on. You know John Holmes. Bit impatient at times." Emily arrived in about fifteen minutes.

"He is a good officer. Trust his instincts. He is ready for anything."

"Well. What is our next move?" Emily waited for an answer.

"I want you and Flanagan to pick up Mama. Bring her to the church. Campbell and I will search for the file. If we find it. We will leave it at that. But if we cannot find it. Mama has to be forced to answer the questions from the past."

Emily turned to Flanagan. "You do know Mama, right?"

"Trust me. She is a bit salty at times. But we can force her to do it. I have a few things on her."

"You salty old dog. Buzz is your cousin." Flanagan laughed. "Most likely my best relative."

Flanagan drove over to the Chain Gang. Parked out front. It was his announcement. It would be a matter of time before she walked out front. A brief confrontation with Flanagan. Instead she held back her anger. Emily and Buzz stood outside to greet her. Mama knew. Emily had a reason to be there. "Good morning Emily, Buzz, of course Officer Flanagan."

"Flanagan is my bodyguard. I am sure. You will co-operate with us. John is waiting for you at the old church."

Mama had little recourse. John Holmes would not tolerate her excuse. It would be easier to face him now. Mama called out. Told them. She had an appointment with John Holmes. It left little to the imagination in the Chain Gang. No one would whisper about her leaving in a police car.

John Holmes admired the ghostly presence surrounding the old abandon church. Thought about the old man and his daughter. So much sorrow and pain between them. The unforgiving menace of the past cast an evil spell on the sacred ground surrounding the church. "Come on Campbell. Time to sit down on the steps and wait for Flanagan and Emily. Our guest will arrive with them."

"Why are we here?"

"Because the old church is hiding a file inside somewhere. I hope Mama will show us. But I also am worried. That the old man has hid it away too."

Campbell whispered. "The sins of our fathers are a far greater sin. Then the words of forgiveness."

"Campbell, I hope you forgive the past. Time to move forward. After all this is said and done. Take some time off. Reflect on the future. Lay the past to rest."

"I guess. It is time to resolve the failures of my life. Figure out. How to move forward. One thing is for sure. My father was not as bad as I thought."

"Strange. How two cases are connected to each other. Mary Jane Hudson and her sister disappear. You father gave away the files. Hoping one day. All this would be put to rest. Now you and I are waiting to find a file. One person I hope will help us. Mama must reconcile the past. Help us to find a file. I am sure. She will resist the confrontation with her father."

"Speaking of the devil. She has arrived."

Flanagan parked next to John Holmes car.

Emily turned to face Mama. "Now is the time to forgive the past. Put an end to this ring of pedophiles and your hate for your father."

Mama. Open the door. Walked directly up to John Holmes. "What makes you think I am going to forgive and forget?"

Flanagan interrupted her. "Martha, I have had enough of your behavior. I can do a tell all."

Mama held her thoughts. "Flanagan, you have always had a way of stopping me. Calling me Martha. Is the first sign of trouble. Tell me why? I am here."

The cast of characters stood silent. Almost laughed.

"Inside of your daddy's old church is a file. Hidden in the walls. John Holmes has the first file. Needs the second one. This charade of killing innocent children from the orphanage must end. Emily will be glad to give a tour of the morgue. Tell me now!"

Mama sat down. Began to cry and ask God to forgive her. Buzz walked over. Sat down and laid his head on her lap. Emily sat down too. The two women talked back and forth. John Holmes motioned for the others to leave. Open the door. They walked down to the front. A sad crying man stared at John

Holmes. Whispered. "God forgive me. For I have sinned against my daughter." Pulled up a broken board on the floor. Pulled a wrapped folder from under the floor. "Time has come today. I have held this folder to long. Heard Mister Campbell passed. I had no one to share it with. So, I buried the past under the floor. I figured if I died. No one would find it. Now the truth shall set those children free. Mister Holmes. Take it and forgive me."

Another voice interrupted. "I forgive you. Emily told me a lot about. What happen and Campbell. Your father did the right thing. Forgive his sins too. Come daddy. Time to go home."

Emily broke down and cried. John held her up. Flanagan reached over and took her hand. Campbell stood motionless. Time would heal a lot of memories. But the truth would be more painful. "Emily, take Martha home. Help her with her father. Buzz you are in charge. Campbell, time to read the files."

Flanagan whispered to John Holmes. "I will meet you later. At least I can share some fore sight on this file."

"Meet me at the morgue. Campbell and I will be there with both files."

Whatever was hidden inside of the files. Would at least reveal the past. Somewhere in time the ghosts of dying children could listen to the sounds of justice.

John Holmes sat down by a steel slab. Rubbed the worn edges of the file. Brushed away the dust and dirt. Never once did he wipe his hands. The dust would be a constant reminder about the past. One by one the papers were turned over and over. Often at times a fist would slam the cold slab. Vulgar words rolled off his lips. Campbell sat patiently. Observing a man reading. Having his heart and soul torn apart. Flanagan returned. Campbell motioned him to be quiet. Buzz sat down beside of John Holmes. Emily witness a man living in sorrow. The pain overwhelmed him. Yet she knew better. Not to interrupt him. Living with his on nightmares. Also reminded him of the past too.

"Emily, how do we help him?"

Flanagan whispered to Campbell. "Leave him alone. When he feels right. You will see him. Hear his voice speak out about the files. The pain and sorrow are his worst enemy right now. Be patient." Flanagan held Emily's hand tight. Observed her tears rolling downward into her palm. "You can't help him right now. He is dealing with a lot of pain."

"Why?"

"Pain of the past is a wound. That never heals. Those children are a burden with a lot of pain. John will settle down. You will feel his pain later. But the police officer inside will take command of his life first. You will have time to love and save him later."

John Holmes closed the file. Walked over toward Flanagan and Emily. "I need you solve a few things inside this file. Flanagan and Campbell, no one outside of this morgue. Is to privy to the file. When the time comes. A lot of people are going down."

John Holmes stood still. Admired Emily and her courage. Kissed her. A simple gesture hit the floor. Buzz ate his snack.

Sound of laughter struck a note of relief. "Okay, Emily get the files. Campbell and Flanagan. See you first thing in the morning back here."

John Holmes held his thoughts. Emily admired his courage. But the lingering thoughts still stood out. Two files filled with hidden information.

"John, what happens here now?"

"Emily, a lot of questions. How will the public and the layers react to these questions? I am sure the shock will rock the state. We are only the messengers. The rest lies in the hands of the federal government and state government."

"It only means that we have fought for an answer. Where will the justice come from?"

"After we make our arrests and prove it. Everything must go public. The national news must bring it to the fore front and call for justice. Every victim is a child. No one should allow this to go away. I am going to put faces on the preparators. I will arrest them and book them. As the lawyers take them out the back door."

"John, I will do my best to insure. The evidence is accurate and honest. No one will get a pass." Emily stared directly into the storm. Law and order stem from the truth.

Mama sat alone. Staring at the past. Tears rolled over the outer edges of her past life. No one knew about the encounter with her father and the old church. Silence held a double edge sword. Began cutting into lost memories of being a young girl. Forced into a situation of being raped. Rolled her palms over and over. Black covered the top of her palms and white was underneath the black color. Very few people every noticed her palms. Yet the scars of time shared the nightmares. Focused on the evil dirty old men took for granted. Yet her heart felt remorse. Reminded her of the harsh world of being poor and black. It was not a division of race. It was the brutal rape of her youth.

Campbell tried to reflect on his youthful life. Son of a police detective. Protected by the hands of the law. Yet he was judged for being the son of police officer. The dark side of life hid a lot his life too. No one knew about the pedophiles. A police department turning a blind eye of justice. Yet the truth dated back through the pages of history. No one ever considered it to be a crime and injustice to young children.

Tom Flanagan sat on the edge of his bed. Staring at the images of his daughter. Wondering how she would have grown up? What would she say to him at night? Remembered the night she disappeared from his life. It was an empty emotional state of failure. A broken marriage followed it at the end.

John Holmes sat down beside Emily. Touched her hand and smiled. "I never dreamed. A day in life would come with an innocent child sitting on a porch. Staring out into space. A burly big dog would protect her from life. Yet a dying man. Who had no reason to care? Left a fingerprint of hope for you. In some ways he was a prefect man. The other side was filled with death. I wonder why? It all happened to him. Then I think you now. I never ever thought about you as a woman. You were a lost little girl with a dog. Now you are a woman with a dog." John Holmes touched her hand and smiled.

Emily sat still. Staring out into space. "John, the day I left you. I turned around. Remembered that one moment in my life. A photograph of my life past and present. I never forgot the moment you handed me a phone. Calling my dad to come and get me. It was a long wait too. But you never left me alone. That image of you standing beside me. Was a photograph I held inside of my heart. Told myself. I was going to find you. To thank you. But my heart felt a lot more. The day I sat in your office. It was worth the day I grew up. Found my dreams to be true. I fell in you love with you that day." Emily leaned over and placed her head on his shoulder. John Holmes held her in his arms and heart.

The days and nights were the pages of time. Filling in the blanks of past lives. A simple bond of hope carried them together.

A reluctant day gave birth to the sunrise. The day before conflicted the truth and life itself. The confusion between life and death was written inside of two files. A journal listing names and dates. John Holmes needed a witness to back the facts. Emily analyzed the deaths of children and one old man. Who was protected and blacklisted? Survived the outcome. Moved into a witness protection program. Still capable of continuing life as a pedophile. Until life removed the connection of his perverted way of life. If anyone had the answers. It was James Winston. A young man seeking salvation and hiding from his past. "John, come here."

Emily began a conversation. Allowing no one to hear. "James Winston is a possible key witness. His uncle used his perversion on him. Fate dealt his uncle a fatal blow. Forced him to become a useless perverted old man. The old man chose a way of life to profit off the souls of orphan children. James Winston is the key to the past and present. I am assuming. He knows the identity of that person.”

John Holmes listen to her argument. Realized he had to consider a choice to attack or leave James Winston alone. John was not a man to sit back and wait for answers to come to him. “Emily, I think we should have an open discussion with everyone here. The input would hurt or change any decision. Unless it proved useful. I want to stop this insane act of perversion.”

“John, I hoped. You would consider it a choice. Everyone here. Is now impacted by the site of dead children. Who died in the past and present?”

Emily spoke first. “I have analyzed the report. I have dealt with the bodies of children. I have investigated Jackson Winston death too. I am beyond the answers as to why? Without your help. I cannot solve this alone. But together. We can piece this all together.” John had to make that one decision to continue.

John Holmes felt her pain. The other two stood silent. Flanagan stepped forward. “Together we can work and solve this. Put a lot of people in jail. Also relive the past and the present to end this insane misery of orphan children. I am in total agreement.”

Campbell spoke. “Time to end the past and the present sins against all children. I am in too.”

“Then it is time to search out a reason and someone else. I want to investigate. James Winston is the one person hiding a lot. He must come forward to help us. Campbell and I will go to the church. Ask permission to talk with him."

Conversation was nonexistent. John Holmes train of thought was about getting to James Winston. How would the church react to him asking to see and discuss his uncle and more? "Campbell, how should we approach the church? Need to get James Winston out of the church."

"John lets, try a straight-forward approach with the head priest. Maybe after all the information he shared. The man may have a conscience and not protect James Winston."

"Maybe. But I am worried about the family's thoughts and ideas of protecting their son. By now James has spoken to his father."

"But James is trying to become a priest. The power of the church is a far greater thing. Would he risk losing it?"

"Campbell got to give you credit for this one. Preying on his weakness and the power of dealing with failure and temptation. Good thought. Time to go find out." John Holmes trusted his instinct. Also figured Campbell being a religious person. Would off insight into the church. Possibly Campbell could induce James Winston to come forward.

"Time for everyone to notice us. Walk around the cemetery before going inside." Sense of sadness overtook both men. The files were now the faces of forgotten children. Sadistic unwarranted attack on faceless children. The graves were not marked. John Holmes anger grew by each step.

Campbell realized. The empty emotions were the faces of lost souls. No one came to take them home. Tears poured from his eyes and soul. Held his breath to keep from screaming.

John Holmes witness the final step of life being stolen from the empty lifeless souls. Having no place to call home. "Campbell, it is time to call out James Winston."

"Time to call him out."

John Holmes and Campbell walked directly into the chapel. John asked to speak with James Winston. Priest left them standing alone. A large door opened. James Winston stepped out into the open.

"I have been waiting or you have to come. I prayed hard and ask god for forgiveness. I was told to answer all the questions from the head of the church."

"I think our conversation. Should be held outside in the cemetery."

James Winston nodded his consent.

The past events of life. Waited for the quest of answers to begin. A sense of darkness hovered over the cemetery. Cool chilling breeze rose from the ground up.

Cold shiver traveled up and down John Holmes spine. Shook it off. Prepared to question James Winston. "I need the information. Your uncle may have shared or things you saw. This is about the past life of your uncle. After he moved here."

James Winston stood silent and breathed deep. "My uncle was a pitiful man after my father did what he did. Broken down and seemed to waste away. But vengeance was in his heart too." James Winston took another deep breath. "Found another way to create pleasure. The one person in his life was a friend. It seems he had found solace in his life. But it was another rogue thought of defiance."

John Holmes patiently waited for him to regain his composure.

"No one knew the man. He had befriended was also a fellow pedophile. In fact. He was a lifelong acquaintance. A man of cloth using the orphanage. To insure his enjoy and lust for power and the bodies of children. But he also knew the story of my uncle's castration. But for a favor in return of using the children to insure his sexual perversion. To be able to fondle them and do other things. He had to provide others to pay for the use of the orphans for sex acts."

"Is this man still in charge of the orphanage?"

"Yes."

"Have a name?"

"Jonathan Morris the third."

Campbell almost fell into shock. "You are talking about the ex-mayor. A wealthy family here in the state."

"It seems the walls of hell have no boundaries, Campbell"

"Did you ever witness these acts?"

"A few times at my uncle's home. Little boys were bought there to be molested by him. It was a secret."

"Can you explain or share any other knowledge of this incident?" John Holmes needed more information.

"Yes. I found a file. I stole it. Used it to black mail my uncle. My father does not know. But you will find incriminating pictures of a lot of people. My father was one of them. He did it. To protect his self from my uncle. After I was molested by my uncle."

Campbell spoke. "Did what?"

"Prevent him from molesting me again. They continued life as it was before. I was a victim of two men." James Winston broke down and cried.

"Will you give me the file?" John Holmes asked.

James Winston opened his coat. Presented the file. "Take it. I have done my duty before god. Not for vengeance. But to find peace with him and the children. I should have helped."

Campbell spoke out in his defense. "James, life is difficult for all of us. Fear can intimidate you. Love for your father is one reason. You tried to protect him. But fear is also painful. You chose the cloth out of hope. I am sorry. But the pain and sorrow will always be a burden. I know."

John Holmes stood silent long enough to allow James Winston to collect his self. "James, go back inside. Speak nothing more of your past. I think you have found your calling. May the blessing of life go with you." John Holmes shook his hand. Allowed Jack Winston to leave. "Well Campbell. You did the right thing. Thank you."

"No. You did the right thing. I found myself today. Thank you."

"Well time to back to the morgue. Face the moocher and his master."

Campbell laughed. "Do mind stopping for a bog of treats?"

"No, your treat today." John Holmes stood still. The man inside of the window signed the cross. John Holmes saluted him.

The bond between two different men. Had been sealed in a peaceful way. Both men forgave each other.

The door seemed sealed with silence. No one spoke as the two men entered. Emily smiled. Campbell gave him a treat. "How is your day going?"

"Flanagan and I seem to have found a roadblock. Jackson Winston died of natural causes."

"Why was he buried?"

"I don't have that answer. But it seems like a way to cover up the death. But the snoop nose detective found it."

John Holmes laughed. "Good job Detective Buzz. Have another treat on me." John flipped him a treat.

Everyone laughed. Buzz calmly ignored them. Chewed on his treat.

Flanagan spoke first. "My guess. It was someone. Who knew he had died? Tried to cover up the death. So, no one would notice. Well maybe until. It was too late."

Campbell made one suggestion. "Maybe someone was trying get rid of the body. Before anyone would notice. To cover their tracks in the investigation."

John Holmes listen intently to thoughts being thrown around the room. "Why would anyone want to do this? It seems so out of place. But then again. It is a sound thought. Considering the man and who he is. Or someone wanted to cover their tracks. To avoid being caught up in the cemetery deaths."

Emily asked one question. "James Winston trying to cover all this up. About his uncle to protect his family?"

"One thing for sure. No one killed him." Flanagan laughed.

"Poor old fooled just pasted and no one wants to claim the body. I guess. We should inform James Winston. About his uncle's natural death." John Holmes just smiled. It was event he had no concern about the old man's death.

In all the joking and laughter Buzz sniffed the body. Sat down. Stared directly at the old man. Flanagan noticed him. "What is up with Buzz?"

Emily turned around to observe Buzz. "Buzz, what are you looking for?"

Buzz sat calmly investigating the body. Ignored Emily.

"I don't like this. Buzz has found a scent. Maybe I should let him finish first."

Buzz walked around the cold slab. Searching and sniffing the area surrounding the slab. Stopped again in the same spot. Stood up on his hind legs. Sniffing the hand of Jackson Winston.

"Looks like you may have missed something."

Emily stood silent. Ignoring Joh Holmes. Observing Buzz at work. Knowing Buzz was intent on finding a cause of death or the area it happened. Buzz pawed at his arm. Until it fell off the slab. Began sniffing at the fingers. Finally sat down in front of the hand. "Emily gave him a snack. "Good boy. You are smarter than any of us."

Emily lifted the arm and examine the fingers first. Separated the area between the fingers. Tilted her head. Pulled a magnifying glass off the table. Pried the fingers further apart. Magnified the areas between each finger. Stood up. "it seems like I have found a needle mark. Test to toxic poisons. Or maybe it was an air injection. Then I will have to search the inside of the heart."

John Holmes stooped over and petted Buzz. Before giving him another treat. "You are a very smart dog buzz. You deserve a bowl of treats. But I have only two left."

Flanagan laughed at him. "Here John." A bag of doggy treats was pitched at him. "Stop by the store on the way home."

"Flanagan, you feed him. I am not being held responsible for that crime of over feeding the moocher."

Flanagan feed Buzz. Observed Emily hard at work. Decided to openly speak to everyone. "Emily please stop, I have a confession."

Emily stood up stunned. "What?"

Flanagan laughed at her. "I did not kill the old man. But I want all of you to listen to me."

Campbell, John Holmes, Emily, and Buzz stood around him

John Holmes listen intently to thoughts being thrown around the room. "Why would anyone want to do this? It seems so out of place. But then again. It is a sound thought. Considering the man and who he is. Or someone wanted to cover their tracks. To avoid being caught up in the cemetery deaths."

Emily asked one question. "James Winston trying to cover all this up. About his uncle to protect his family?"

"One thing for sure. No one killed him." Flanagan laughed.

"Poor old fooled just pasted and no one wants to claim the body. I guess. We should inform James Winston. About his uncle's natural death." John Holmes just smiled. It was event he had no concern about the old man's death.

In all the joking and laughter Buzz sniffed the body. Sat down. Stared directly at the old man. Flanagan noticed him. "What is up with Buzz?"

Emily turned around to observe Buzz. "Buzz, what are you looking for?"

Buzz sat calmly investigating the body. Ignored Emily.

"I don't like this. Buzz has found a scent. Maybe I should let him finish first."

Buzz walked around the cold slab. Searching and sniffing the area surrounding the slab. Stopped again in the same spot. Stood up on his hind legs. Sniffing the hand of Jackson Winston.

"Looks like you may have missed something."

Emily stood silent. Ignoring Joh Holmes. Observing Buzz at work. Knowing Buzz was intent on finding a cause of death or the area it happened. Buzz pawed at his arm. Until it fell off the slab. Began sniffing at the fingers. Finally sat down in front of the hand. "Emily gave him a snack. "Good boy. You are smarter than any of us."

Emily lifted the arm and examine the fingers first. Separated the area between the fingers. Tilted her head. Pulled a magnifying glass off the table. Pried the fingers further apart. Magnified the areas between each finger. Stood up. "it seems like I have found a needle mark. Test to toxic poisons. Or maybe it was an air injection. Then I will have to search the inside of the heart."

John Holmes stooped over and petted Buzz. Before giving him another treat. "You are a very smart dog buzz. You deserve a bowl of treats. But I have only two left."

Flanagan laughed at him. "Here John." A bag of doggy treats was pitched at him. "Stop by the store on the way home."

"Flanagan, you feed him. I am not being held responsible for that crime of over feeding the moocher."

Flanagan feed Buzz. Observed Emily hard at work. Decided to openly speak to everyone. "Emily please stop, I have a confession."

Emily stood up stunned. "What?"

Flanagan laughed at her. "I did not kill the old man. But I want all of you to listen to me."

Campbell, John Holmes, Emily, and Buzz stood around him

"Remember Mary Jane Hudson. She actually is alive." Flanagan smiled. Offered no explanation about his thoughts and expression concerning the truth.

"Where is she at?" Emily was shocked and wanted to hear the truth.

"I told you to ask Mama. She has covered up the actual truth." Flanagan offered the information.

John Holmes never questioned the merit of Flanagan's thoughts. For some odd reason, he knew it was the truth. "Flanagan, what does this have to with you now?"

"I found her late one night. She was beaten almost to death. I called Mama."

Sudden appearance of James Winston changed everything.

John Holmes stood silent. Holding his anger and thoughts. Wondered why? At this very moment would James Winston suddenly appear.

Emily observed the stone-cold face of man. Who would do nothing to try and stop a criminal in his tracks?

Flanagan recognized. John Holmes would pounce on him in a heartbeat. "James Winston, why would you? Want to stop by the morgue? Do you have a reason for this visit?"

Emily blocked John Holmes. "James, I think you need to confess to the truth. If you know? What happen to your uncle? Someone killed him." Emily probed his weakness. Knowing the well of being priest feared being shamed.

James Winston stood silent. Fear slowly engulfed his thoughts. Sight of John Holmes staring directly into his eyes.

Never speaking to him. Was a very intimating experience. "What do you want me to say?"

John Holmes walked over and stood face to face. "For once in your life. Time to face the truth. Well?"

At the age of twenty James Winston had never faced a man. Hell bent on the truth and justice. The golden spoon of life was mired in death and fear. "I am not sure. If I tell the truth? What happens?"

"The truth could set you free. A lie could put you away. Tell me. Which one?"

Sadness engulfed the young man. Realizing it was a moment of truth. Having to choose between the church and family. Yet the solemn moment between life and justice. Hung an albatross around his neck. Tears rolled over the edge of his eye lids. Also flashed back into his conscience. Trying to avoid the moment of truth. Almost wanted to lie. Fabricate a story of not having any type of knowledge.

John Holmes stepped up. Sat a soda down on the desk. Without ever saying a word. Sat down staring at the floor. Before looking up to search the eyes and soul of a confused young man. Trying to choose his fate. "Difficult moment in life. When you have to choose one over the other?"

"Yes sir, it is."

"Are you trying to consider the fate of your religion over the facts? Are you concern with the outcome of telling the truth? Are you thinking about the ways the truth will hurt someone close to you? It seems like passing judgment is a far greater task than forgiving a sinner. Do you need more time alone?"

"No sir. I am weighting the sins of my judgment. How many thoughts? It will take to choose between life and death. All of which will affect some one's life. One way or the other. Not an easy task to predict." James Winston had hung a huge yolk around his conscience.

John Holmes realized. In one moment of an honest conversation. A young priest was about to confess a sin or share the sinful truth. About an entire community within the boundaries of life and the city too. For the first time in his life. Asking questions about the outcome between life and death. Hung in the balance of James Winston's conscience as a priest. A long deep silent thought creeped over his conscience. Feeling like an intrusion of a confession before a man would be put to death. Yet he held the same silent moment before the confession would haunt him or relieve the stress of his own choice to serve one master. In one simple hand movement. Brushing away the tears of heaven. James Winston kneeled upon his knees and prayed in silence. John Holmes witness a humble servant of God. Questioning the morality of his life and soul to serve one master. Yet he also wondered. Would he serve the devil or god? John Homes turned around to avoid eye contact. John Holmes stood at the door. Thinking about the other side of life.

James Winston whispered a prayer. Before turning his soul to the reality at hand. "Detective Holmes, I have a confession to make before my god and you."

John Holmes stood silent almost in shock. Yet he wondered if James Winston's confession would lead to a conviction or a folly of religious faith? "Are willing to speak freely.?"

"Yes sir, it is my duty as a man of the cloth. To protect the youthful souls. That have been discarded into a grave. Without anyone willing to save their innocent lives."

John Holmes silently sat down. Took a long deep breath. "You do realize your fate will be questioned under an oath and lawful society within the boundaries of a court. So, there for I must ask if you need a lawyer and read you your rights to protect you."

James Winston sat silent. Finally, after a long pause took a deep breath of air. "Yes. I understand. Perhaps you should find someone to write this all down. It will take a lengthy time."

John Holmes sat stunned. Before he finally answered the request. "Let me make a call for someone." John Holmes dialed the court for a someone to record the statement. After a fifteen minute wait a young woman arrived. She sat up her equipment. Tested the microphone and recorder. After a run through and test. She explained his rights and the action about to taken. Explained to John Holmes that he could start and stop any conversation as needed to protect the young priest from being convicted on the evidence. As he spoke.

"Okay, James Winston, do you understand your rights. As I have given you before you start?"

"Yes."

"I am not going ask you any question. This is not a confession. It will be a legal document concerning your views as you have stated before me. You may ask to be a witness too. If you speak of any criminal offense. I will give you. Your rights to have a lawyer present. Do you understand?"

"Yes."

"I am going to have make a statement and we are going to record your statement. Are you ready?"

"Yes."

"I want you to start from the beginning and move forward to the present day. I am going ask you to describe the details you remember. I will not interrupt you. Unless it requires me too. I want you to start and describe the events and time period in which it happens? Tell me the first time. You were aware of the sexual behavior in your life?"

"When I was a young boy. My uncle molested me. My father found out. One night my father walked out of the house. Gone for two or three days. Returned as if nothing had happened. I assumed it was a business trip. My dad had my uncle castrated for what he did to me. I lived in silence and was confused at first. But as the years pasted. I grew a custom to my dad's trips. Never question his wellbeing or life. But as the years passed by. Heard rumors around school and town. The rumors suggested my dad had sexual relations with young girls. The business trips were side shows for his craving to have sex with little girls. My thoughts of a father being a great man. No longer existed. But the other rage was hearing of exploits and the other wealthy members of men. Having a club built around the same type of stories. Then one day I witness the outrage. Campbell's father would bring underage girls to parties in the bottoms.

Stood there crying and begging to go home. Only to be raped by dirty old men with money to buy them. It was an extension of perversion and protecting the boys club from the law. My father found displeasure in my life. I found God and the church. I am not proud of my life. But I am here to resolve the sins of a family and other children. Who suffered death and more?"

"How much does Mama know about all of this?"

"I am only one voice. I cannot speak for her. But she knows more than she is willing to share. The bottoms are covered with dark secrets from the past. Your quest for the truth began with Mary Jane Hudson. The molestation of the past and your judgment is clouded with images. Temptation is a greater sin than the actual truth."

"James Winston a manmade god of wisdom. Hiding behind his past and using the cloth of the church. Weaving tall tales to coverup the actual truth behind his image. Tell me Jack. Where do you fit in? The fact of your thoughts and words are not always the truth."

James Winston was stunned by the thoughts of John Holmes. "What do you mean by that?"

"You fit a certain word in the thoughts of a police officer. Who are you trying to con? Those little twitches. Looking down the floor. Never once did you look me in the eyes. Should I just ask you the questions one by one? You are acting like a runaway child."

James Winston broke down and cried. John Holmes flipped him a box of tissue. Sat down across the table from him. Patiently waited for him to regain his composure. John Holmes knew from the beginning that James Winston was conning him. A short deposition and lack of evidence proved worthless. "First question Jack. Did you want a lawyer?"

"No!"

"When did your uncle decide to rape you?"

"I was seven and it last several years before my father found out,"

"What did your father do then?"

"Confronted my uncle. It was about five days later before I found out. What my father had done to him."

"Did you father do it or someone else?"

"My father paid a doctor to do it. Someone back east a friend. I think."

"So, you do not know the truth about the incident?"

"No."

"Have you ever had sex with another child?"

"Yes. I was thirteen at the time."

"Was it, consensual sex?"

"Yes, I am gay."

"Why are you telling me this?"

"It isn't about me. My father is a pedophile too. He had sex with my sister and other children."

"Why are you telling me?"

"Because I watched him. The others have children buried out there. When I saw the police digging it up. I knew. My conscience would get the best of me. So, I pretended not to know."

"What about Campbell's father?"

"His father help provide children for the others."

"Does anyone in the church know your gay?"

"Yes. We are lovers. No one inside knows."

"Did you murder your uncle?"

"No."

"Do you know" Who did it?"

"No. My uncle had a lot of enemies. He constantly black mailed them for money."

"Are you willing to testify in court? Will you help bring these people to justice?"

A long silence hung over the air. The balance of justice waited to be tilted in one direction or the other. James Winston was the only one. Who held the power to tilt the pendulum of truth and justice for every child's body? That was found in the cemetery. Sound of silence was broken. The shattering sound of a sigh broke the silence. "I want to be protected for the information. For what I am about to share. It will shatter both the church and the city too."

"Where are you going with this? I want the absolute truth. This time!" John Holmes would no longer. Be put out by the outrageous contempt to change or hide the truth. James

Winston was a key witness to the obscene sickness of raping children. For the pleasure of a grown man's sickness to appease his lust. The timetable of life was poison. The lives of the past had been buried under a cloak of darkness. The vengeance came from the silent movement within a cemetery. There were no walls or praises asking for forgiveness. God's walls of faith hid behind the same dark clouds. "Well?"

James Winston sat still. Gloom filled the air over the dark circle of tears. Almost sitting in a crucified position with his arms draped over the edge of a chair. Silently waiting for lightning bolt to strike him to death. But the wages of sin and the church silently waited for a confession and the truth. "If I seek forgiveness and open my heart and soul to condemnation. I will be crucified by the church. If I lie to protect the church. My salvation will not be god's forgiveness. The faces of angels covered with the deadly sins of some one's filthy hands for their sinful pleasures. I must confess and bare my sins before justice. God's children were victims. Preyed upon and sacrificed for the demons within the black hearts lusting to prey upon their victims. Give me a pen and paper. I will write a list of the names, time, and places. I will be excommunicated from the church." James Winston sat in silence.

John Holmes laid a pen and paper on the table. Sat down across from Jack Winston. Waited for the hands to start writing. After one hour and ten pages later. A compile list of dates and names pushed back into the direction of John Holmes.

John Holmes lifted the papers and began a tearful search. The painful heart break of the unforgiving sinful men. Who lusted for the bodies of innocent children? Turned around and handed the pages to the secretary. "Make copies for me. I will keep a complete confession of this in a private folder to protect it from the eyes of those. Who may try to protect their names on this list? You will return with a recorded record of James Winston confessions and records. Stand up James Winston. I am placing you into protective custody. For the time being. I will take you to the church. To gather up belongings. After warrants are delivered. There may be an attempt on your life. Do you understand me?"

"Yes sir. I do. But it will make no difference one way or the other. I will be betrayed and crucified before God and his sinners. My death is Imminent."

"Not if I can help it. Besides someone owes me a favor. I am about to collect it. I need to make a call. Sit down." John Holmes took out his phone. Push the speed dial. Listen for a soothing comfortable voice to answer.

"Hello. You have been gone a long time. Safe to talk?"

"Go to Mama. Tell her to wait inside of the Chain Gang. I need her to protect someone from the injustice of a crime. Text me back and stay with her. Tell Flanagan to protect her."

"I will text you as soon as I have her in my sights and no one is around. Love you." Emily looked down at Buzz. "Come big boy. Time to go to work."

Emily sat stoned face. While driving to the Chain Gang. Buzz laid down in the passenger seat. Quiet and humbled for some odd reason. Buzz scent caught a reason to be solemn and patient. Emily noticed the concern on his face. Patted him on the head and nose. Flipped a treat to him. Buzz calmly chewed it up.

Finally sat up. Searched the outside world. Piece by piece he finally realized. He was at the Chain Gang and the scent of food exposed his timely weakness for a larger snack. If a big black nose ever knew the scent of a place to eat. It was Buzz. He patiently sat still waiting on his master to open the door. Emily smiled at him. Swatted his butt before opening the door. Buzz being obedient to his master. Sat still waiting to get out. Just to rush into the kitchen for a free hand out. Emily open the door. Walked with Buzz to the front door. It was a great moment to see him play wag the tail for a full course dinner. In all the amusement Mama sat in a corner. Staring directly at Emily. Emily took little or no concern for the shifting eyes. Preying upon her emotions. Instead walked a straight path to the table and sat down uninvited. Mama brushed the cold silence. Snapped a finger and had a plate brought in for Buzz. "Is this business or pleasure Emily?"

"John asked me to stop by. He will be arriving soon. Needs your help." Emily offered nothing more. To many eyes and ears around the table.

"No problem my child. How is my favorite customer doing with that meal?"

"Mama, if he came every day. I would not be able to drag his fat butt up the steps. It is okay, not any daily trips. No more-large portions." Emily smiled and petted the chow hound.

Mama smiled. "I hear things are not good at the cemetery. To many children buried there. You know a long-time ago. Perversion of this type was no secret. Be it girl or boy. The church profited off such a thing. Turned a blind eye to any type of molestation. It was not forbidden."

"Mama, a lot of things were allowed. Marrying your daughter to someone at the age of thirteen was legal. First cousins were legal. During the sixties it was legal. A husband could rape his wife at will."

"Yes, white men could rape black women and little girls at will, no crime was committed according to the law. What is the difference?" Mama felt the heart ache of life. The emotional break down of being black. Without a hint of justice from the past or present.

"There is no difference. Rape is a crime now. But the claims of the past. Never cover it. The past will always be a lie. Now someone will pay for the pain and suffering."

"Who will and when?" Mama never shed a tear from her painful thoughts. That were connected to the past. But the present-day murders were enough to connect to the past events.

"Mama, tell me about the past in this town." Emily politely tried to squeeze information from a pasted era of time. Hoping Mama would at least try and explain the evil from the past.

"Child, you will never understand the truth or the reason for the crimes of the past. I know a lot of things. Some things should be left alone. If you do not leave it alone. Death may come to call upon your home and life." Mama lived in fear of the past and felt no concern to change the present-day history.

A shadow cast itself over the table. It was John Holmes with James Winston in tow. "Why the sudden shock on your face?"

"Because you have come for a reason with a snake in tow. Why is he here?" Mama spit at John's feet.

"If you want the truth? Then expose the lies and tell the truth Mama. From the beginning of all this and the murder of Mary Jane Hudson. You have stone walled my efforts for the truth. Now take me to the bottoms. Let the chips fall. Where they may fall. If anyone there is guilty of the sins in that cemetery. Then I am going arrest them." John Holmes spit at her feet. The entire restaurant sat still. No one spoke or whispered. Silence was the moment of truth. All eyes were on Mama. The power she willed was now under attack.

Mama walked over to John Holmes. Emily sat still in the moment of truth and justice. Yet at that one moment Hemingway wrote about in a book called 'For Whom the Bell Tolls'. Created a sense of failure and the truth between the law and the will of one woman. "If I expose the past and show you the truth. Will you protect the ones in the bottom?"

"You have my word."

Emily stared into two sets of eyes. Forever a moment of truth meant the failure. Loss of innocence for everyone to see. The world would be changed in the eyes of the beholder and the lair. Yet the pages of time began to open it page by page. The silence fell upon the dead victims. Who had no voice in their deaths? Which now had been placed in the hands and mine of one woman, Mama.

Mama sat still. In one passing moment of her life and future. Came in view of her world and the people. Who worshipped and relied on her protection? The bottoms would soon know the reasons and answers for their judgment in one fell swoop. Mama for once in her life. Wished to free of the bonds. The people she protected from the outside world. The Chain Gang could only whisper and assume. The woman, who protected them from the very evils of life. Was facing the unexpected truth and her judgment day. The symbol of John Holmes presence was a reason for uncertain events. Were about to create an unknown disturbance inside of the Chain Gang. A brief engagement of silence would sooner later turn into the thunder. No one wanted to hear. The expression on John Holmes facial muscles were stern and stone.

Mama stood up and raised her hands. To silence the whispers. Sound of a pin falling would resemble the crashing thunder before a storm. Mama finally breathed out and spoke. Loud enough for everyone to hear and witness. "John Holmes, you can thank Emily and Buzz. She shared her thoughts. Spoke the words of truth, justice, and wisdom. I cannot change history. Tonight, I will help you to John Holmes to change the silence of the past. It will ring loud for years to come. I will take you to the bottoms. You will hear the voices. That have been forgotten."

John Holmes knees trembled. The sound of truth proved to be the final moment. That would solve the crimes of children. Whose unknown disappearance. Would finally find justice and peace. "Mama, I promise. To do my best to solve and protect the people. Who have suffered the most and punish the criminals?"

James Winston witness the one unexpected moment in life. No one wanted to hear the truth. It was about to become a reality. What would happen now? The disbelief of the thought of being involved in the deaths. Has risen to a higher volume of regret and hopeless emotions of the young priest.

John Holmes stared directly at the crowd of people. It was eerie to see and feel the heart break of so many people inside of the Chain Gang. For one moment in time. The name of the restaurant proved to be true. How many of the black people staring directly at him? Had family members serving time and dying on the chain gangs of the past. Turned around to look into the eyes of the past and present. It was the only pair of eyes. Whose relatives were part of the despicable behavior toward anyone. Who could be raped and molested for the pure pleasure of being able to do it? James Winston closed his eyes out of fear.

John Holmes whispered to him. No one knew or heard the conversation. Silence ensued throughout the moment of silence. Between two men, one with honor and the other hid behind the only honor. He had. A velvet cloak of disgrace. It held the blood of a crucifixion.

Mama witnessed the perfection of murder. Being held higher than her own black magic. But the devil had no witnesses to protect the wicked sounds being spread across the Chain Gang. She whispered to John Holmes. "Time has come to leave the deadly presence of righteous souls. Turning into a lynch mob."

John Holmes acknowledge it. "Time to leave Emily, Flanagan and time for all of us to leave this mob behind."

Pure thought of death proved to be a perfect time to rush out into the darkness. Mama as always provided a wedge between her and the ones. She left far behind to protect her thoughts and beliefs. No matter the thoughts or hopes of so many lives. The pages of time and sins. Had begun to change the face of a town. The past was about to shed the truth upon a bleak dark history in time.

COME UNTO ME

The shadows between the darkest moment in people's lives. Are the moments of truth creating a painful reality? Forgiveness is not a willingness for a heart and tortured soul. It is a moment in time. When the tears of a broken soul are set free.

John Holmes stared into the darkest moment of time. Tears rolled over and over the edges of his eyes. Emily witness the broken heart of a man. She fell in love with. A warm soft tissue of life touched his hand. Held on tightly. A simple moment of compassion. Did not distract from his love and pain. But touched the bond of love. Held between him and Emily. He smiled. Squeezing her hand. Simple moment of compassion also bonded their love.

Mama admired the young woman. Saw the true depth of compassion and love. It reminded her of the conversation earlier in the evening. Emily truly was the compassionate woman. Who had found a place in her heart and life for one man?

Buzz laid silent. Admiring the scents of the bottom. A place for a dog to feel free. Yet the same reminder also alerted his senses. Business came before pleasure.

James Winston sat quietly wishing for a moment of peace. As the pages of life felt the fiery rage of hell burning. Well inside of his faith.

Campbell admired the emotional scenes of life unfolding before his eyes and thoughts. No matter the outcome. A vast spell of darkness would soon answer a lot of anger and the truth. Between the pages of his life and the packet of disgrace forged from a father shielding his self from a crime. Left an empty pit of life inside of his lost soul. But the fate of life also brought a new chapter. It was just beginning to unfold.

Un-natural occurrence appeared. Fog coated the wilderness along the path filled with broken souls. No one in the bottoms knew that John Holmes was preparing to prove that a foundation of sexual rape was now on trial. Mama sat quietly. A single bit of moisture touched her cheek. Another part of her life proved more painful. The woman was also a victim of powerful society forcing children to be sexual slaves. From the ashes of forbidden sins, she rose from the ashes of pain. Ruled the bottoms, protecting the broken souls within in it. Who refused to live in shame and pain from a cruel world outside of the bottoms?

Sun rose upon the quiet foundation of life within the bottoms. No one expected their lives would be turned upside down. Put a on a public stage to be tried for the sins from the past.

Mama walked. Along the center of the bottoms and realized the scent of life was empty. The faces of the people were no longer broken-down humans. It was a shameful disgrace of misery hiding from the tortured soul of a broken-down human being. John Holmes and Emily patiently walked behind her. Empathy was bound by the sorrow of life. Was created to torture the ones, who found no justice in a crime. That they felt and never committed. Yet life rose above all the other things. Within the barriers of time peace and hope grew from the ashes of the past. John Holmes almost walked away. But Emily held him to his word. Everyone had to face their demons. Emily knew. How difficult it would be. After leaving Christopher Robin's house. She still had to face the reasons. Why she ran away. But she also found compassion and the gift of life. From her family and friends. But her greatest strength was her father. A teacher and compassionate man, who loved his children. No matter. What she had done. He forgave her. Taught her to enjoy life. To never be a shame of failing in life. It was only a lesion of being a child. Who would grow up one day and feel the same compassion? She smiled and realized that the same man. Who shared the last day of her captivity? Would be the same man, she fell in love with.

A familiar face greeted John Holmes. Jacob hugged him. Held his hand. "Can I walk with you today?"

Mary stood silent. Admired her son's courage to encounter the man. Who shared part of his life with him?

"I don't see. Why not. Do you remember Emily and Buzz?"

"Yes."

"Why don't you and Buzz. Sniff around for things to do. Take him over to buy a treat. He is hungry." John Holmes decided to protect him from the investigation.

"I see you have given Buzz a new way to be a bum. I am so greatful you saved him from all this." Emily hugged John. Buzz playfully enjoyed the company.

Mary sensed something was wrong. "John, you protected my son from the reason. You are here, why?"

"Time to set you free. The crimes of the past have no place here or anywhere. I must find the truth in order to protect all of you. Change the outcome of the past." John Holmes touched her hand and squeezed it.

"You should also leave the past alone. There is a great deal of suffering too. Maybe the past will disappear once and for all."

"Mary, take a long look at Mama. Did you see her suffering and pain? She has suffered a long time to protect you and your son. Set her free and forgive her pain and sorrow too." John

Holmes needed Mary to speak out in her defense too. "You need to speak out too. Stop hiding the past too."

"Mama told me to never speak about the past. It was to protect me from the pain. You want me to tell you the truth, why?"

"Because a cemetery is full of young boys. Some are forty years old. Some are less than a year old. We found a newborn baby covered in dirt. What can I say to convince you?" John Holmes found his self-begging.

Unknown to them. Mama overheard the conversation as she walked closer. "Mary, I have lied and cheated the world out of the truth. I have protected you from the past. To save Jacob from the pain. James Winston's father raped your mother. You are his half-sister."

Emily rushed over toward Jacob and Buzz. "Come on you two. Time to get some morning ice cream." In one instant Emily had saved Jacob from the worst possible thing in his life. Together all three walked in the opposite direction.

Mary stood silent. A single tear rolled down her cheek. Mama reached out to comfort and hold her. James Winston almost passed out. Campbell grabbed his arm. Whispered to him. "Life is a bitch. Reality is a place called hell. Welcome to your past. How do you feel about life in the presence of god?"

James Winston bent over and puked. Used his sleeve to wipe away the stench of life. Began to mumble a prayer asking forgiveness for his sins.

"Remember the things we did together. To hide. Who and what we were? We had to hide it. Played the game of life to hide all this emotional credence of failure. Come on James tell the truth for a change. Tell John Holmes the truth. Stop pretending you found salvation. How many kids have you raped? Was it a great feeling? Did your father teach you too?"

John Holmes witness Campbell becoming unhinged. Rush over. Shoving him back away from James Winston. "I must advise you of your rights. If Campbell is telling the truth."

Mama and Mary almost passed out. Never in one moment of time. Had she seen two full grown men engaged in saving and punishing the same crime in the name of God. But the aftermath of any decision will determine the failure of one of them.

"Mama, what has happened to cause so much hate and pain?"

"Mary, the world as you know it. Has collided with the truth. So much that the history of the past has caused the present to collide with the truth. You may witness. Is all I can say. I must share your past with it too."

"But I do not know the past. I am living here. As I have always been. You raised me to believe. Who I am? Is it a lie?" Mary almost wanted to cry. But her faith was stronger. She also wanted to protect Jacob.

John Holmes witness the pain and suffering unfolding. Realize the truth was a painful fact. No one considered the outcome. Before starting the investigation. But death also opened the past. The scar of time carried consequences too. From a baby covered with dirt to fifty years of unmarked graves.

"John, it is too late to stop it. Mama will not allow the truth to be buried now. We must be prepared to face the past and the present. It may take a hundred years to heal the scars of history."

For Campbell it took a lot longer. Growing up in a house built around the confessions of crooked cops. Protecting the wealth and riches of white privilege. Hiding an unknown fact of life. That was unacceptable in his father's eyes and soul. Never did he ever imagine that being a police officer. Would create a world filled with a darken past of sadistic cops preying on children. No one ever outed or spoke of the disgraceful society of wealth. Enjoying the flesh of children. Unable to defend their selves. Observing the values of poverty and being held hostage. Realized a man would sale his soul to feed his family. Yet he never witnesses the deaths of the orphans the church sold. Until the day the bodies were discovered.

An old black man walked over toward Campbell and James Winston. Stopped staring at the two men. Thought, about the outcome. In a split second he spoke. "Jesus died on a cross to spare the world of its sins. Satan smiled. Surely you jest about salvation and forgiveness. Open your eyes. A far greater sin is your death. But who am to judge a sinner?" Without hesitation he turned and walked away.

"One can only wonder about the thoughts and expressions of an old black man." Mama heard the words. "Simply told the truth." John Holmes heard Mama. Thought about the words of an old black man.

"Mama, have I crossed the line down here. Is the truth worth the pain and sorrow. It will create down here in the bottoms."

"John, I fear the painful sorrow of the past. I am afraid of the truth. But the time has come today. If I do not embrace the truth. Who will care about the people? Long after I have gone from here. How dark does the truth have to be? Before the words have meanings. No, John. But before I can preach a sermon on the past and future. I must tell Mary the truth too. Ask Emily to take Jacob away from here. She must protect him from the truth. I must share with his mother." Tears of sorrow flowed over her cheeks. For a far greater tragedy occurred. The life of a young woman. Would also suffer the pain and sorrow of justice.

John Holmes hugged Mama. Whispered in her ears. "I am sorry for the pain. I have caused you today. Please forgive me too."

"Go the truth has set you free. Tell Emily the child bares the fruit of the future. Let us not hear or suffer from the truth today. Protect his innocence for me." Mama prepared for the pain and sorrow. She was about to expose Mary too. It would be difficult to explain a long-hidden secret from her past.

Emily walked away from the fate about to unfold. She also remembered the days of her captivity. But time healed the past. She found peace and happiness. "Come on Jacob. I smell some good treats around here. Time to go party."

Jacob smiled. "Are you serious?"

"I sure am. Are you hungry?"

"Yelp, how about Buzz?"

"Buzz is always hungry. He eats like a horse. Then wants to sleep. We may have to walk it off with him. What do you think?"

"Oh, I have a few cool things. We can do. Buzz will enjoy it too."

"Come on the party is way over there in the treat store of sugar and spice."

Mama and John Holmes smiled. "Emily loves children. You got yourself a wonderful lady."

"How did you know that?"

"The twinkle in her eyes. Tell all about the way a woman loves a man. You are a different man now." Mama punched him in the gut.

"Mama, Are you sure about this?"

"Yes, time has covered the truth long enough. I must set her free. It will cause pain in the heart and soul. The anger will fade with time. Do you realize. How many others will suffer from the truth? How will we save and comfort all those people and the women and children? Who died and suffer at the hands of perverted old men?"

"God help us. I have no way to explain it. Much less the faith in my conscience to prove a right makes it wrong too."

"John, too late to turn back. I have hidden my soul and sorrow too. I want to cry and scream. But I also see the faces of the past. Who cry for justice? All those poor children. Having no voice at all. Who died in a house of sin and pleasure?"

"I cannot argue against the truth and you at the same time. But I can justify the reasons. I am doing this once and for all. Someone must be punished for a crime. It is the law."

"John time for us to walk the streets. Ask for one and all to speak out against the abuse and tell their stories. Explain the pain and suffering. Turn no one away for any reason at all. We can sort out the message, time has given us."

Together for two days Mama and John Holmes search for answers and witnesses to prove the abuse. It was not as simple as anyone would have thought. Some shied away from the pain. Others refused to be a part of the past. Yet through of the pain and sorrow. The gray voices of time spoke out. About the abuse and deaths of the young boys buried in unmarked graves. Most painful part of all. Were the names of the ones buried in the cemetery. An older worn wrinkled face of time bared the scars of time. Remembering a younger brother begging for help. Listening the screams of pain and sorrow. As the acts of rape continue hour upon hour. Saddest the moment of all were the tears of fellow orphans suffering for the failure to save their brothers or never seeing the face of young boy never return. One by one the empty faces of time were being written in a warrant. A warrant to arrest the co-conspirators. Who committed a crime against, humanity and a defenseless children? Only to be buried in an empty nameless grave. The temple of God stood silently watching. Approving of the acts of murder against defenseless children. The final testament proved to be the hardest. Mama had to explain the reason why Mary was raised in the bottoms.

John Holmes knees trembled. Mama calmly walked beside the police officer. Holding her pain and sorrow within her soul. Before the final confession of truth. Would be spoken to a young woman. Who was unaware of her past? Emily held John's hand. Walked along the side of him. Tears rolled over her cheeks.

Found it to be difficult to be present at the confession of a woman. Who finally had to face a child? Who grew to be a woman and parent of child?

Mary stood alongside of her son. Held his hand tightly weaving a firm grip to protect him. She heard all the rumors. Listen to painful confessions of the lost after their confessions of knowledge about the past. She kneeled beside of Jacob. "Jacob, big mama is coming. It is our time to face the truth. I want you to leave with Emily. I have too. Speak with John Holmes and Mama alone. I want to protect you from the past. When you become of age. I will tell you the truth. Until then I want you to remain a child. You have not grown old enough to hear or accept the truth. But one day you will know the truth. I promise. Now go and take Emily's hand. Walk Buzz until you cannot hear a voice." Placed a finger over his lips and kissed his forehead. Pushed Jacob toward Buzz and Emily.

Emily smiled. Motioned Buzz to escort Jacob. Buzz pushed him around like a soccer ball. Never allowed Jacob to turn around. Instead played a game of tag. Nipping at his heels. Jumping and running away. Sitting down daring Jacob to catch him. Emily used this technic to amuse children. During a trauma situation to avoid pain and sorrow. It liberated their sorrow. Creating a situation of a basic conversation. As the game was played out.

Mary enjoyed the playful behavior of Buzz. Turned around to face Mama. "Mama, the time has come. To deal with the hidden past in my life. I am not ashamed of the past. I hope."

Mama hugged Mary. Held her close to her heart. Whispered. "I am sorry. But I have to share this moment."

John Holmes stood back to allow the two women to hug and cry. Purity would prevail in a moment of truth. Justice would be nothing more than a band-aid. Time for a period of compassion and love. Would be the only cure for the events unfolding between the two women.

Mama turned back to face John Holmes. "John, I want you and Mary to hear this. Mary Jane Hudson was your mother. Her father pimped her out at age thirteen. Through the years she was beaten by him. For refusing to share herself with the pedophiles in this town. He almost beat her to death. I found her on the side of road. Picked her up. Bought her precious life to the bottoms. She gained her heath back. She was pregnant with a child. You were born Mary. She stayed with you for three years. One day she disappeared. Leaving me with a loving note. To raise and take care of you. I never found her ever again. I am sorry. But you and I have to bring that old man to justice."

Mary cried. Never spoke a word. But another voice step forward. James Winston asked to speak in defense of Mary Jane Hudson.

Mama stood in silence and shocked. John Holmes stood and waited for Mary to answer the question. It was her choice in life to find the truth and justice for mother. No one else would be allowed to make this decision.

Mary simply wiped away the tears and pain. It created an emotional moment in her life and Jacob's life too. "If I am to learn the truth. It will solve the mystery of my mother's life. Then please tell me the truth not a lie."

James Winston stood up right. The action of being a priest entered into his soul. A moment to gather his soul and be humble occurred. Taking Mary's hand. Softly began to speak to her about her faith and hope. "Mary, I am a priest. I live at the church. Right now. A moment of truth has opened a door. To many children have died at the hands of evil men. But one day a young woman appeared at the church. She was scarred by the brutal beating from her father. Yet the elegant lady held her courage up. She begged to hide inside of the church from her father. A man. Who had almost beaten her to death? The priest inside opened the door. Beckon her to come inside. Provided a room for her to live in. Never one word was ever spoken about her presence there. She works daily to clean and serve the meals for all the priests. Your mother has a beautiful soul. A tattered worn out picture is inside of her heart and the bible. I hope you understand the great sacrifice. She made to protect you from her father. But now you have a chance to see her. Forgive her for being the perfect mother. She made Mama promise the day she left to raise and protect you from her father. I beg you. To come meet the mother. Who sacrificed her child to protect her from a disgraceful old man? Who used and battered his daughters for money?"

John Holmes silence and a stunned looked. Almost broke down and cried. The simple pride of a rugged tough cop almost fainted. Yet his hate grew stronger. No longer tempted to stop the hunt. But to arrest each and everyone involved in the murder and rape of children.

Mama held her up. Mary's knee buckled from the truth. She tried to speak but could only cry. Realizing her mother was still alive. She hugged Mama and the priest. Pulled herself together. Finally spoke. "Today. I feel as if a great painful burden of life. Has set me free. John, Mama, Emily, and James. I need to see my mother. She needs to meet her grandson. Please take me to her today."

James Winston turned back to face John Holmes. "Please help her and her mother. Time to reunite them is here. I will be witness to all the crimes. I have seen and have knowledge to save this woman and her son."

Emily spoke. "John, time for the truth. Let this child become a child with a hope and dream. She has sacrificed more than anyone."

Mama clutched his hand. "Time to finish this once and for all. I failed to share the truth. About all the things within this mess. If you must punish me too. I will give testimony too."

The darkest cloud of truth and justice. Had been held hostage for over fifty years. The empty souls of lifeless orphans died for the sensual pleasures of wicked old men. A century of rape and murder of black women and children had been hidden in tainted white pages of history books.

John Holmes stood silent. "Today justice will be served. But first a child and her child will finally be reunited with her mother. I will guarantee the protection needed to save them from the past and present."

James Winston finally answered for a lot of disrespect of his family. It proved that he no longer was in the shadows. But lingering questions still existed. It would be something for him and John Holmes to solve together.

Campbell stood silent out of respect. But the lingering quest for respect and approval was still unanswered.

John Holmes walked over to Campbell. "Do me a favor Campbell. Be sure and protect James Winston from leaving or going anywhere for now. This day is a long way from over. You and I have a crime to solve and finish."

"Yes sir. I will make sure of it. Thanks for trusting me again."

John Smiled. Emily observed the quality of a police officer. Doing his job and protecting everyone from the events unfolding.

"Attention everyone. Time to move from the bottoms. Emily, you and Mama meet us at the church. Mary, you and your son will travel with Buzz, Mama, and Emily. All right everyone follows me to the church."

The bottoms seemed empty. The long disgrace of the past changed the pages of the history. Life and hope returned for the people living in the past. A sense of hope replaced the darkness. Finally, a shade of life and the truth appeared inside of hopeless lives. Long forgotten from the past decades of time. But the final moments of the past had not been opened yet.

The doors of the church hid more secrets than the world outside of it. Yet the moment of truth would share a forgotten moment of the past. A young woman who had locked herself away from the past. Had grown older. The youthful face was tired and empty. Scars lined her cheek bones. But the polite older woman was a strength within the order of God's temple.

No one spoke words of her past sorrow. But were pleased to escort her around and help. James Winston lead the small group forward into the past. A slender grey-haired lady hummed as she worked. "Good day Mary. Do you have a moment to chat with me? I have a few guests. I hope you will guide them on a tour of the church."

It was an awkward moment. "James, I would be pleased to do it."

James smiled. "Thank you, please walk with me. I will introduce you to my guests." James took her hand. As he had always done in the past. Too comfort her.

She saw only a small group of people. Smiled and welcome them. "Hello Mama."

Mary Jane Hudson stepped forward and hugged her. "I missed you so much. Please forgive my tears."

Mama and Mary cried on each other's shoulder. No one interfered in the reunion.

"Come with me. I want you to meet my friends." Mama took her hand and walked up to John Holmes. "This is Detective John Holmes, Emily, and Buzz. Please sit down on the bench." John escorted her to the bench. Held her hand as he sat with her. "Why are here John?"

"I am here. As a guest of someone. A young lady and her son want to meet you. May I have the honor of introducing to them too?"

"Yes, please."

Mama escorted Mary and Jacob over. Mary smiled. She began to cry. "Oh my god. My beautiful daughter is here. I bet you are my wonderful grandson too" In one moment of time. Love found a passage. Pulled a lost soul from her prison cell.

"It is time to come home. I never knew. Who you were? Take my hand and Jacob's hand. Mama, Emily, and John, please help my mother. I want to take her home."

Mary Jane Hudson stopped. "Please walk with me. Someone else here. My sister is here. I saved her form my father. I think she will enjoy having a family too."

Mama and Emily laughed. Mary spoke. "I think. We will love having another beautiful person in our life. What do you think Jacob?"

"Yelp. My grandmother and an aunt. All in one day."

Perhaps one moment in time proved that an ounce of forgotten love. Set a woman free from her past life. The images faded from her broken heart.

John Holmes stood silent. Watched the past fade away. Felt the time spent in the bottoms was worthy of being remembered by a man. Who was once tortured by the loss of his wife? He found the compassion of life sitting on a doorstep. Calling her parents to take her home.

Emily turned around. Buzz sat by John Holmes. Smiled at the two most important loves of her life.

Campbell witness the greatest moment in his life. For once his father never got to force anyone to stop.

John Holmes turned his attention back to James Winston. "For once in your faithful life. You did the right thing. Restored the love and compassion of a woman. The world had forgotten. After a long investigation into the past. She is with her daughter and grandson. But one thing remains. You and Campbell and I are going to arrest an old weather-beaten old man. He deserves his fate. Then I will determine the fate of your life."

James Winston stood silent. Finally accepted his responsibility as a priest. "My life and future are in your hands. I accept the terms of my actions."

"Campbell time go visit old man, Hudson. Time for the piper to pay for his crimes."

Emily realized. John Holmes was about to force the hand of the truth. The will of a town would be shocked and twisted into a nightmare. Long overdue from the pages of time and history.

John Holmes stopped out front of his house. Hudson sat on the porch in a rocking chair. The house was tattered and worn down from the age of time. It seemed time had not been good to the old man. Unfortunately, the past was about to catch up with him and a few other perverted pedophiles.

The old man coughed. "Well, looks like the long arm of law. Has finally come to call upon me. I heard all the stories. Going around town. You know. I am too old to convict and spend the rest of my time in jail. The jury will determine that to be true."

John Holmes smiled. "You know. Mister Hudson, I have a witness. Who may disagree with your thoughts? You do remember Mary Jane Hudson, right?"

"Hell, she has been dead for a long time. You got no proof." Spit at John Holmes feet.

"James Winston and Officer Campbell. Tell him the truth."

James Winston spoke up. "Mister Hudson, Mary has lived in the church for all of her life. But a miracle happened in the eyes of the lord. Her daughter came to the church. Set her free of her bonds. You created. The day you almost beat heat her to death."

"Officer Campbell advise him of his rights. Help the damn fool to the car. Lock him up. Call the state to get him a lawyer. Would not want to deprive him of his rights."

John Holmes turned to face James Winston. "If anything. You found a place to forgive your sins. The sins of your father. You will never be forgiven by your family. But I know one thing about life and the bible. Remember the lord said come unto me for forgiveness. You proved it to be right. Campbell give the priest a ride home. I am sure he is missing mass."

John Holmes turned to Emily. "Do you mind if I make a stop on the way home?"

"No, as long as it doesn't take long."

John Holmes smiled. "Want take too long to stop by the hospital. Got a call about a baby. Make sure everything is all right."

"Is anything wrong with him?"

"No. Just a stop by for the nurses. You can visit him too."

John drove quietly to the hospital. Never once spoke a word. Emily felt quite worried by his mannerisms. "Okay lady.

Let us go visit the little monkey." He laughed. She slapped him on the arm.

John and Emily walked down to the maternity ward. A group of nurses waited for his arrival. Head nurse asked Emily to hold him. She smiled and talked with him. He just giggled at her words.

"Well, what do you think of the dirt baby? He has grown quite a bit."

"Oh, you are such a beautiful baby boy. I wish. I could keep you forever."

Nurses all laughed at her. "Do you have a name for him?"

"No, I never thought anyone would ask."

John laughed again. "How can you take a baby home. If he does not have a name."

Emily cried. "Oh my god. I love you. As for you little one. I will call you. John Robert Holmes. But Robbie will be your name. I do not want you two to be confused. Thank you. John, I love you."

John Holmes had finally found love and peace within his life. The angel of the past smiled down on him. Mick proved to be a wonderful angel in his thoughts. Under his breath. He whispered I love you too Mick.

Robbie laughed. Emily kissed him. Buzz sat in the car. Wagging his tail.

John Holmes remembered one thing in life. His mother told him. Remember the things that hurt the most. Are the gifts life someone share with you. God will say to you. Come unto to me. I will forgive you and mend your broken heart and soul.

SUM OF ALL REASONS

Sand of time drip one by one in an hour class. Pages of life are written on the wind. Love is held inside of a lost soul. Seeking answers to the forgotten past. Compassion of forgiveness is the key to all the reasons. You take for granted as a child.

Dedicated to the lost souls of life. Never turn the page of life. Until you for give your past. Love the ones you lost in life.

Hope is not eternal. It is a part of living life.